Meg didn't feel like a stranger in Steve's arms.

In fact, she felt practiced and confident kissing him. She didn't care that Steve Hartly was completely and positively wrong for her in every way. She kissed him with all she had, refusing to harbor any negative thoughts.

Too soon he pulled away, leaving her lips bare and wanting. Meg's heart thumped against her chest. Steve made her feel womanly and out of control all at the same time.

Why had she returned his kiss with such fervor? She needed him to help her, not kiss her. If she could get him to practice medicine again, he could save her clinic. She wanted to keep everything aboveboard—shove her physical needs out of the way.

Hoping to clear her mind, she breathed in the rich, thick morning air. Even in her confusion she knew one thing.

She wanted to understand Steve Hartly.

Dear Reader,

March roars in in grand style at Silhouette Romance, as we continue to celebrate twenty years of publishing the best in contemporary category romance fiction. And the new millennium boasts several new miniseries and promotions... such as ROYALLY WED, a three-book spinoff of the cross-line series that concluded last month in Special Edition Arlene James launches the new limited series with A Royal Masquerade, featuring a romance between would-be enemies, in which appearances are definitely deceiving....

Susan Meier's adorable BREWSTER BABY BOOM series concludes this month with Oh, Babies! The last Brewster bachelor had best beware—but the warning may be too late! Karen Rose Smith graces the lineup with the story of a very pregnant single mom who finds Just the Man She Needed in her lonesome cowboy boarder whose plans had never included staying. The delightful Terry Essig will touch your heart and tickle your funny bone with The Baby Magnet, in which a hunky single dad discovers his toddler is more of an attraction than him—till he meets a woman who proves his ultimate distraction.

A confirmed bachelor finds himself the solution to the command: Callie, Get Your Groom as Julianna Morris unveils her new miniseries BRIDAL FEVER! And could love be What the Cowboy Prescribes... in Mary Starleigh's charming debut Romance novel?

Next month features a Joan Hohl/Kasey Michaels duet, and in coming months look for Diana Palmer, and much more. It's an exciting year for Silhouette Books, and we invite you to join the celebration!

Happy Reading!

Mary-Theresa Hussey

Mary-Theresa Hussey
Senior Editor

Please address questions and book requests to:
Silhouette Reader Service
U.S.: 3010 Walden Ave., P.O. Box 1325, Buffalo, NY 14269
Canadian: P.O. Box 609, Fort Erie, Ont. L2A 5X3

WHAT THE COWBOY PRESCRIBES...

Mary Starleigh

Silhouette
R O M A N C E™
Published by Silhouette Books
America's Publisher of Contemporary Romance

To Susan McKeague Karnes, Liz Lounsbury,
Tina Oldham and Donna Smith, fellow writers,
who challenge, inspire and support.

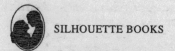 SILHOUETTE BOOKS

ISBN 0-373-19437-4

WHAT THE COWBOY PRESCRIBES...

Copyright © 2000 by Mary L. Schramski

This edition published by arrangement with Harlequin Books S.A.

® and TM are trademarks of Harlequin Books S.A., used under license. Trademarks indicated with ® are registered in the United States Patent and Trademark Office, the Canadian Trade Marks Office and in other countries.

Visit us at www.romance.net

Printed in U.S.A.

Books by Mary Starleigh

Silhouette Romance

What the Cowboy Prescribes... #1437

Silhouette Yours Truly

The Texan and the Pregnant Cowgirl

MARY STARLEIGH,

born in North Carolina, is a ninth-generation Southerner. She claims her Southern background is where she acquired her love of romance. "I adore creating characters who are brave, honorable and find true love."

She writes full-time, teaches English and creative writing part-time at a small Texas college and mentors high school students. Her husband, a pilot, reads all her romances. They have one daughter.

IT'S OUR 20th ANNIVERSARY!
We'll be celebrating all year,
continuing with these fabulous titles,
on sale in March 2000.

Chapter One

"Sunshine needs a doctor."

Meg Graham jumped at the desperate words and her heart thumped hard against her ribs. Cal Bradford's scared face stared back at her. She stood and grabbed her medical bag. "Who is it?"

"Erin Waldron."

Meg pushed past Cal, sprinted out of her office and clinic, and down the sidewalk to the Sunshine Café.

Out of breath, weary, and fighting a feeling of dread, she pulled the door open and rushed into the restaurant. A stranger was kneeling beside Erin. The man's dark gaze was filled with concern and he was patting the healthy but frightened child.

Meg steadied herself by inhaling deeply.

"Listen, little guy, you choked because you didn't take your time chewing."

The man's compassionate tone filled Meg with relief.

Erin nodded. "Yeah, I know."

"Thank you." Sue Waldron was standing close by her son. "Erin and I were on our way to get feed for his horse...and we just stopped...thank you so much."

Sue's voice broke, and Meg slid an arm around her shoulders.

The stranger stood and gazed down at Meg. He towered over her. "Erin'll be fine. I've checked him."

"Come on, Erin, we'd better get home," Sue said.

Mother and son collected their belongings and headed for the door. Erin turned around and waved. "Thanks, mister."

A smile and deep emotion graced the man's face for a quick moment, then vanished.

Meg gripped one of the Sunshine's red plastic chairs. "I can't thank you enough. I'm Meg Graham, Jackson's only doctor." She stepped forward and extended her hand.

"No problem." He nodded, shook her hand quickly, then turned and walked to his table. After placing a few bills by his check, he shrugged into his jacket and headed for the door.

"Hey, wait a minute. I'd like to know your name," Meg called as she crossed the room.

As if not hearing her, he opened the door, stepped outside and pulled it closed behind him. Meg stared at the door for a moment, then grabbed the knob. She yanked it open and walked out into the Texas sunshine.

The man pivoted back toward her. Furrows gnarled his forehead and a look of pure aggravation darkened his handsome face. Chestnut hair, the color of a wild horse she'd ridden once, was combed back from his forehead. A black turtleneck accented his tanned skin and was tucked neatly into new jeans that had been pressed to a knife's edge.

Her hand found his arm, and the rich, soft cashmere of his jacket. "At least tell me your name so I can thank you properly. Are you a doctor?"

"I was."

"And your name?"

"Steve Hartly."

His dark, smoky voice wove a spell around her. "Are you just passing through Jackson?" she pressed.

"I stopped for lunch."

The color of his eyes, like dark Texas earth, again reflected the strong emotion she'd seen inside the café, when he was comforting the child.

Meg's hand dropped to her side and she took an exhausted breath. "Thanks for stepping in and helping Erin."

Steve studied her for a moment, then jammed his hands into his pockets. "You're welcome. But there's no need to thank me. It was a simple procedure."

Before she could say anything else, he turned to leave.

Her hand flew to his arm again. At the touch, his biceps hardened, and butterflies fluttered in her stomach.

He turned back. "I need to get going."

Meg caught a glimpse of their reflections in the mirrorlike, plate-glass window. Steve was at least a head taller, and the painted yellow heart on the café's sign was accenting both their shimmering images.

Another fluttering of butterflies assaulted her.

"It's tough being the only doctor in town," she blurted. Now why had she said that?

Silently he studied every inch and curve of her body, then glanced into her eyes. "You look like you can handle just about anything."

As if on the wild horse again, Meg felt her stomach flip-flop.

"Well...y-yes," she stuttered, confused at her physical reaction to the stranger.

"I've got to be on my way."

For some crazy reason, she didn't want Steve to leave. "Sorry your lunch was interrupted."

"No problem." His right brow arched slightly,

making his face more asymmetrical, yet more handsome.

"Sunshine has great food. You'll have to..." The rest of her suggestion evaporated. What *was* she planning to say?

Steve brought his hand to his chin and studied her again.

"You might want..." Meg was finding it hard to complete a thought. "My office and clinic—" she pointed down the sidewalk "—right there...."

She glanced back to the reflection in the café window. Why hadn't she combed her hair earlier?

His brow arched again.

"Ever practice in a rural area?" she queried.

Steve shook his head.

"Well, it's very interesting. Busy, though. Jackson's a wonderful place." She poised her hand on her hip. His eyes remained on her, and her mouth turned as dry as a Texas wind.

Darn it!

What was wrong with her? She'd felt so tired before she'd come down to the Sunshine, yet at the moment she was feeling so alive. Maybe all she needed was a good night's sleep.

The sun came out from behind a feathery cloud, and Steve squinted a little. Tiny crinkles formed around his eyes and added to his attractiveness. There'd be no sleeping with this man around. Coming from out of nowhere, the thought jarred her.

Steve cleared his throat. "I should get going."

Before she could say another word, he walked to a shiny black BMW sitting two parking spaces down from the Sunshine Café. His muscular legs carried his massive frame with ease.

Meg leaned against the concrete wall and crossed her arms. Steve opened the car door and climbed in. Through a lightly tinted windshield, she could see him settle himself against the seat and start the engine.

Then his attention shifted to her. His strong jaw accented his full mouth, and one dark brow arched higher than the other again, adding to his powerful, mysterious persona.

Meg's stomach fluttered once more. She was either hungry or tired, and right now she couldn't do anything about either state. She gripped her arms in a self-conscious hug, then raised her right hand and waved goodbye.

Steve didn't smile, only nodded, then maneuvered the soundless automobile out of the parking space onto Main Street.

She chewed the inside of her cheek and shoved her hands into her pockets. Thank goodness that was over. But she was glad he'd been around to help Erin.

Cal Bradford opened the café door. "Hey, Meg, can I buy you a cup of coffee?"

"No thanks, Cal. I've got to get back to the office. How's Donna?"

"She'll be okay if I can keep her from working so hard."

"You need to make her stay off her feet. It won't be too long now until you're a daddy."

Cal smiled and then shook his head. "You know Donna when she makes up her mind." He shifted his gaze to the street. "Good that guy was here."

"Yes." She gazed at the last trace of shiny black metal. "Don't let Donna work too hard, Cal." Meg nodded to him and started down the sidewalk to her office. She only managed to take a few steps before she glanced over her shoulder.

The black BMW had disappeared.

Hopefully, her afternoon and evening would be less disruptive than the past ten minutes had been.

Three hours later, Meg sat behind her desk, closed her eyes and wondered how long a person could actually go without sleep.

"You okay, Mego?"

She glanced at her cousin and held out the letter she was still holding in her hand. "My insurance company says I need another doctor for the clinic."

"So go out and hire one," James Dean Pruitt stated in his matter-of-fact way.

His innocence made her want to laugh, but the aching fatigue attacking her every muscle wouldn't allow Meg even a chuckle. She shook her head. "I tried to find someone last weekend when Jackson almost fell apart without me."

"Kate and I figured you went to Galveston for a long weekend. Not so, huh?"

Meg waved the letter again. "For weeks I've been trying to find a doctor who'll work in Jackson. This bureaucratic memo from my insurance company gives me no choice now."

"How so?"

"They're demanding I find another doctor or they're pulling my malpractice insurance."

"Can they do that?"

"Sure. The suits at the home office claim that with my high doctor-patient ratio it's unsafe for me to run the clinic." From a tiny reserve of stamina, Meg found the energy to laugh. The entire situation seemed so ridiculous. Not one physician at the Rural Conference for Doctors in Dallas had been interested in practicing in her hometown.

Her head throbbed and her body ached. If she were her own patient, she'd order herself to go straight to bed for three days. Maybe this was how people really lost it—never getting a decent night's sleep and then careering straight off the deep end.

"Nobody wants to come to Jackson?" James Dean's question shifted her attention. He frowned.

"Not one. I'm still the only doctor for seventy-five miles." She brought her hand back to the desk and thumped the golden oak with her knuckles. "I even paid my own way to Dallas. Do you have any idea how much hotel rooms cost in that city?" She brought her hands to her face and rubbed her temples with the tips of her fingers.

James Dean rose from his chair, stepped over to her desk and rested his large palms on the only space not covered with papers. "Mego, you're gonna wear out real quick."

She inhaled a defeated breath at his realistic words and cradled her chin in laced fingers. He was right. In the past few weeks, she'd made mistakes from sheer exhaustion. She'd caught them all, but it was starting to spook her.

"I still can't believe John left…and for *money*. I'm trying to take care of his patients *and* mine. One human being can't do it all." Being a small-town general practitioner gave new meaning to the word *busy*.

"Something has to give," James Dean said.

"A lot of things will give. If I don't find someone in a month, I'm going to have to close the clinic."

Her cousin straightened, crossed his arms and stared down at her. "You can't do that. We need you."

"And I can't run the clinic without insurance. That would be professional suicide."

"Folks aren't going to like driving to Fort Worth. How about Charlie's asthma?"

"I know," Meg whispered. She massaged her temples again. She'd treated James Dean's son many times for a mild case of asthma. "Too bad the doctor I met at the Sunshine Café isn't sticking around."

"What?"

"Erin Waldron choked on a piece of hot dog down at the café. A doctor who had stopped for lunch helped out."

She'd sign Steve Hartly up in a minute. A laugh slipped from her lips. She wondered how he'd like working in a run-down, dusty Texas town.

"Something funny?"

"No. Just thinking about a man I met."

"About time." James Dean's eyes gleamed.

"It's not like that." But with only the brief memory of Steve Hartly, the silly butterflies were back. To fight them, she turned her attention to the letter on the desk. "What am I going to do?"

"If it's money...Kate and I could scrape up a few bucks."

She looked up at James Dean, loving him for the offer. "It's not the money. That's the least of it. I need a warm, breathing body attached to a medical license, someone who just happens to be living in Jackson."

Steve stared at the cracked kitchen sink, then turned, walked into the living room and glanced around. Every window in the house had been broken out.

He owned a certifiable, unlivable dump.

That hard fact, on top of the emergency in the

café during lunch, grated on his nerves. He'd vowed never to touch another patient again, but when he'd seen the child choking, how could he *not* help? And the doctor he'd met after had thanked him so nicely.

An image of Meg Graham paraded through his thoughts. Her open, pretty face and expressive, chocolate-brown eyes still grabbed at his gut. The desire to see her again oozed through his body like warm syrup.

Steve danced the beam of the flashlight over the walls of the living room to distract himself from thoughts of Meg.

Why did I have to stop for a meal where there was a medical emergency?

An autumnlike breeze whipped through the broken windows and fanned across the living room to the kitchen, causing the screen door to squeak.

He wasn't even sure where to begin repairs. The Realtor had said it was a fixer-upper. Spending the past five years of his life as an emergency-room doctor had prepared him to repair broken bodies, not plumbing or drywall.

Steve crossed the carpetless floor and stepped onto the small front porch. He gazed at the orange-streaked sky spreading to the far horizon. Its beauty was foreign to him. In Houston he'd never had time to enjoy sunsets.

The sound of a car and the flash of headlights coming down the lane brought his gaze around. A GMC utility vehicle kicked up pebbles as it turned into the only other driveway on the small stretch of road.

Must be his neighbors coming home. Maybe they'd know someone he could hire to replace the windows in the house. Then, at least, he wouldn't have to sleep in his car for more than a few nights.

Taking the three small steps all at once, Steve lunged off the porch, hoping his new neighbors were friendly.

Chapter Two

Meg clicked on the kitchen light and set her grocery bag on the counter. She glanced at the wall clock above the stove. If there were no emergencies, she might get a decent night's sleep.

If she could sleep.

What in the world was she going to do about the demands of the insurance company? There were no quick solutions. And to top it off, the incident at the café this afternoon had rattled her more than she liked to admit.

The tall, handsome image of Steve Hartly danced slowly through her exhausted thoughts. She couldn't put her finger on what, but there was something very different about him.

She puffed out a deep breath.

Something different, indeed. She'd practically hyperventilated when she'd looked into his eyes.

Meg chuckled. Even as bushed as she was, she could still fantasize about a good-looking stranger. She shifted her attention and gazed out the window.

"What a stranger," she whispered. He was unique, but strange? No. She'd felt quite at ease with him even though he hadn't said much. And in those few short moments, she'd sensed he had some kind of worry on his mind.

Meg shrugged her shoulders. Oh well, she'd never see him again. She crossed the kitchen and stopped to check the answering machine. The green light held steady, thank goodness. She tapped the beeper attached to her waistband as if knocking on wood.

This afternoon she'd finished her office appointments, returned all telephone calls and completed her house visits. For the first time in three weeks, she was caught up on everything except sleep.

Maybe if I splash my face with cold water, I'll feel better.

Back at the sink, Meg turned on the faucet, cupped her hands and splashed cold well water onto her face in an attempt to relieve the soreness in her eyes. Then she patted her hand on the counter, in search of a towel.

Darn! All her towels were in the hamper with the other laundry she planned on doing. As she straightened, droplets of water ran from her face and hair onto her collar. A knock brought her gaze to the locked screen door.

Steve Hartly stood on her back porch, outlined by the wooden frame, his image blurred by the gray mesh of the screen.

"Oh!" Meg's heart raced against her ribs, her breath coming in quick puffs. Why was *he* standing on her porch out in the middle of nowhere?

"I didn't mean to startle you." His deep voice carried across the room to her.

"What in the world?" Meg's chest heaved and her hand fluttered to her heart.

Steve's expression turned to sheer surprise. "I saw a car...but didn't realize it was..."

"What are you doing here?" Maybe he *was* strange. He could easily have waited and followed her home. The thought quickened her heartbeat, causing her chest to tighten.

"I saw a car and figured it was my neighbor." Steve rested his hand against the doorjamb and squared his shoulders. Even through the screen the man looked extremely handsome.

"Where were you when you saw me?" Meg reached for a paper towel and patted her face dry, her heart still stampeding. At least the screen was locked.

"I own the house down the road." His left hand went to his head and he scrubbed his hair with his fingers.

"You bought the *Lemon House?*"

"No."

"If you bought the house down the road, then you own the Lemon House." She pressed her fingers against her lips.

How in the world could he live in that dilapidated old place? And right down the road from her. She drew a wooden kitchen chair out from under the table and sat down.

He nodded. "Oh, Lemon House, right. I get it."

"Everyone in town calls it that." She stood. "Sorry I didn't ask you in. Blame my bad manners on surprise." Meg walked to the door, unlatched it, then pushed it open. "Please, come in."

Steve filled the entire door frame with his brawny physique. Grime and dirt covered his jacket. A wave of sympathy rolled up Meg's spine. The Lemon House's condition was probably worse than she imagined. It had been years since she'd even been inside the abandoned place.

"Can I offer you a cold drink?"

"No thanks." He looked around her bright kitchen.

"I didn't think anyone would buy that old house."

"I failed to ask the Realtor for details." He smiled a little, and her breath caught in the back of her throat.

She stepped back a tiny bit and looked up at him. Steve was taller than she'd realized. "You don't plan on staying there, do you?" The idea of him living in the falling down house didn't sit comfortably with her.

"I came over to see if you know of a repairman. All the windows are broken out...." He squared his shoulders again.

Meg held back a smile. It was hard to believe anything could daunt Steve Hartly. She studied the pained look on his face and another wave of sympathy moved through her.

"I might know of someone who can help you. Please, why don't you sit down?" She found her own chair at the table.

Steve joined her and folded his hands in front of him. The fact that he wasn't wearing a wedding ring intrigued Meg.

Her gaze moved to his, and she found him staring at her. "Welcome to the neighborhood."

"Thanks. Anybody else live around here?"

"Just me...and now you."

The worry line between his dark brows deepened.

"Are you going to make some of the repairs yourself?" Her heart thumped hard in her throat. The man sitting across from her seemed to undermine her self-possession.

"I was planning on making the minor ones. Now I'm thinking about just renting a bulldozer and..."

"Oh, it can't be that bad. Besides, Jackson has a great hardware store. Down the street from the café. Bowden's. Family-owned. Saturday nights they sponsor a country-and-western dance at the Sunshine Café. People come from miles around to dance and have fun.''

''I'm not sure one small hardware store is going to have all the supplies I need.''

The man had such a sincere voice. She drew an invisible line on the table with an index finger, then shifted her attention back to him. ''I haven't been inside the Lemon House in years. Pretty bad?''

''Yeah.''

''I hope I thanked you properly for helping Erin.'' She hadn't talked to another doctor casually in a long time, and right now, it felt remarkably good to sit across from Steve.

''No need to thank me again.'' His left hand curled into a fist, his knuckles growing white. ''Just doing what any doc—anyone would do if they could.'' A dark look swept across his face.

''What if I had been out of the office and you weren't there?'' She stopped when his look grew more troubled.

''It worked out. That's all that matters.''

''Yes, I guess you're right. Sometimes I worry. People in Jackson are good folks. I do my best.''

''I can see that.''

Meg's hand swept through her damp hair. Steve raised his eyebrow for a moment, then brought an index finger up to his mouth and rubbed at his lip. Worry lines began creasing his forehead again.

''Are you looking to practice medicine around

here?'' she asked. Maybe he'd be the one to help her.

"No.'' The thin, quick denial sliced the air.

"Retired, at your age?''

"I'm not practicing anymore.''

"Oh, you'll go back. I'd never be able to give up my practice, leave medicine.''

Steve's eyes narrowed as he stared at Meg. "No. I won't.''

"Burned out? You probably just need a break.''

"I need to get back to my house.'' He slid his chair back and stood.

Meg gulped. She couldn't let him leave now. "Wait, I'm too nosy, sorry. It's just nice to have another doctor to talk to.'' She got up and smiled. "Let me get you the name of the someone who'll help you.''

"I do need the number, but—''

"Cal Bradford does repairs and construction. He has a new baby coming in a few weeks. I'm sure he needs the work.''

Steve crossed his arms. "Maybe that's not such a good—''

"He does great work. Wait till you talk to him. I have his number in my book.'' She quickly stepped to the small kitchen desk, glad for the excuse to put space between herself and her guest. Being so close to him caused her to feel slightly off center, almost nervous.

"I don't want to bother you." He uncrossed his arms and moved toward the back door.

Crazy, mixed-up thoughts whirled in her mind. Steve Hartly was a doctor. Through her exhaustion, excitement rippled. She hoped he'd have at least half a dozen years of experience under his belt.

"Wait, Steve! It's no bother. I'll get you Cal's number." The man standing in her kitchen might be her last chance.

And she wasn't going to let Steve Hartly get away so easily.

Steve watched Meg walk to the desk against the wall. Above a stack of papers hung an ancient rotary wall phone. Her delicate fingers flipped through the pages of a personal phone book. She snatched a sheet of notepaper from a stack and scribbled a number.

His gaze drifted. The stark white shirt she was wearing accented her gleaming brown hair, which turned up in a sexy flip at her shoulders. The silky strands shimmered, seeming to have a life all their own.

While she thumbed through a large stack of papers, Steve let his gaze slip farther down. Her worn jeans hugged her well-rounded hips and emphasized the curves of her perky bottom like the skin of a very ripe tomato.

He swallowed hard. Although he had more important things to think about, he couldn't take his eyes off her nicely rounded backside.

Meg turned around and he jerked his gaze up.

She cocked a dainty eyebrow, telling him she knew he'd been giving her the once-over.

"Here it is. Give Cal a call. I'm sure he'll help you." She handed him the piece of paper.

He studied what she'd written. Her handwriting—a small, rounded script—was as well proportioned as her figure. A drug company logo embossed the top of the small square sheet. It jolted his memory. He'd prescribed their medicine many times to patients who suffered from high blood pressure.

His finger traced over the raised logo. What he'd enjoyed most in practicing medicine for five years was helping his patients adopt healthier lifestyles...

Steve pushed back the feelings that needed to stay in the past.

"It's not too late to call." Meg's words broke into his thoughts.

"I don't have a phone. I'll drive into town tomorrow."

"You can use mine. But I'm surprised you don't have a cell phone."

Her eyes were almost the same color as the shiny mahogany furniture he'd purchased for his office in Houston, then sold three weeks ago for a tenth of the price.

"I got rid of my phone." Before he'd left the city,

he'd sold all his possessions except his car and clothes.

"Oh. Well, use my phone, then. Anytime." Her lips broke into a wide grin and dimples formed in her cheeks.

"No, I'll wait." The urge to outline one of the small indentations with the tip of his finger made him uneasy, then suddenly overwhelmed him.

"Cal does need the work. You'll be doing him a favor."

Her genuine kindness made him want to crush her to his chest and kiss her soft lips. Instead he stared at her. A smudge beneath her right eye caught his attention. Before he could stop himself, he reached out and traced it gently with his index finger.

Her long, lush lashes feathered against his skin and his breath came in ragged spurts. Meg's eyes widened and he counted five full respirations before she pulled back.

"There's a smudge under your eye. It's still there."

Meg felt her hand tremble as she brought it up to her face. Steve's fingers were warmer than she'd expected. She rubbed hard at her skin. "Did I get it all?" She glanced down and wished her hand would quit shaking, but she knew it wouldn't while his eyes were holding her captive.

"Yeah, it looks like it."

Steve turned his head slightly, and Meg noticed a

tiny heart-shaped mole on his jawline. She nibbled her bottom lip and forced her gaze to his jacket.

"You're so dusty. What did you do, climb into that old fireplace?"

Steve brushed at his coat, causing tiny clouds of soot to float in the air. He studied her for a moment. "No. I got this from just walking around the place. Why's your hair wet?" His fingers caught a wayward strand, then let go.

"I splashed my face, hoping it would make me feel better. I'm exhausted. Remember med school? Eyelids grainy from no sleep and feeling like hell? Guess that's how my mascara got where it's not supposed to be."

Meg brushed back her damp hair, wondering how bad she really looked, and upset with herself for caring.

"Med school…seems like a long time ago." Steve cleared his throat. "There's not enough time to learn everything."

"I felt the same way. But then eventually everything slides into—"

"Sometimes. I'd better get going." Steve folded the note with Cal's number in half and slipped it in his coat pocket.

Meg shifted. She couldn't let him leave. Even though she was really tired and apprehensive, she had *plans* for Steve Hartly.

Chapter Three

"**W**hy don't you use my phone?" Meg positioned herself between her guest and the back door. "It's a shame to wait. Besides, you'll make Cal's day." She gazed into Steve's dark eyes and, before she knew what she was doing, rested her hand on his arm.

His muscles tightened under her fingers.

"No. I can make the call tomorrow."

Meg brought her hand away. "Please. I enjoy your company. Go ahead and call."

"Well, if you're—"

"Good. I'll get us something to drink." She motioned toward the telephone, and the tension in his shoulders seemed to ease a little.

"I guess it would be easier to call from here."

"Of course it would. Then you can relax, drink

some iced tea.'' Meg stepped to the kitchen counter and started unloading groceries. She'd all but forgotten about the milk, eggs and bread.

Steve went to the phone and dialed Cal's number. Soon he was talking about the Lemon House. Meg filled tall glasses, then sat at the table and waited for him. When he hung up, he picked up Charlie's inhaler and glanced over at her.

''Asthma?''

''Not me. My cousin's little boy. The child is always losing it. I'll take it back in the morning. Just put it by my purse.''

He did as she asked and turned back.

''So was Cal happy?'' She took a sip of her tea and glanced at him over the rim of her glass.

''Says he can start tomorrow.'' Steve leaned against the back of the chair.

''Cal will do a great job. His wife is having their first baby in a few weeks. Oh, I told you that.'' Meg took another sip of her drink. What was wrong with her? She usually never repeated herself. ''Donna works too hard around their ranch. She's healthy, but I've delivered her sisters' babies, and they've all had difficult deliveries.'' Steve's expression tightened and he shifted as if he were uncomfortable.

Meg waved toward his glass. ''Sit down and have some tea. I made yours plain. You don't use sugar, do you?''

''No. Thanks.''

''So how long did you practice?''

"Five years."

"Me, too. I did a one-year residency at Presbyterian in Dallas, then came back to Jackson. Been here ever since." She tilted her head nervously. Steve was the type of man who listened—and watched. The type who made her feel...was it uneasy, nervous or what?

Her temples pounded. Why, for goodness' sake, had she told him about her residency? He hadn't asked. She needed to bring the conversation around to *his* medical practice and not talk about herself.

"I was raised in Jackson." The information seemed to spring from her mouth.

He picked up his glass. The man sitting in front of her had a way of making her feel all mixed up. Although he was quiet, she guessed he had a wonderful bedside manner, serene and calm.

The last thought stunned her. She wasn't really thinking at all about medicine. In just the blink of an eye, Steve Hartly was making her envision soft down comforters and cold winter nights snuggling under them—with him.

"I was born in Jackson." Good Lord, hadn't she said that? "I mean, uh, and I've lived here most of my life except when I went away to school. You practiced how long?" She'd already ask him that, too. The man was going to think she was an idiot! Quickly she vowed again to keep her mind on finding out more about Steve Hartly.

He placed the glass on the table and drew his finger through the beads of condensation.

"What kind of practice did you have?" she asked breathlessly.

"I worked the emergency room for four years." His tone had gone flat.

"How'd you pick Jackson?"

"Wanted a place far away from Houston."

"Know anyone here?"

He shook his head. "Just looked at a map and made a few phone calls."

"Do you miss the ER?" Good. She was getting some great information. Yet it bugged her that she really liked the idea of finding out what made him tick, what caused the faraway look in his dark eyes to come and go.

"I try not to think about my old life." His finger lingered on the glass, then traced around it again, this time in the opposite direction. He didn't bother to look up.

"I know how you feel. Like today. I panicked until I saw you in the Sunshine. And I worry about Donna all the time, afraid I won't be there for her. I just have to put the worries out of my mind. Sometimes I feel like I don't know what the heck I'm—"

"Being a doctor is not all what's in here." Steve tapped his right temple, then reached across the table. His index finger stopped an inch short of her chest. "It's what's in your heart that counts."

His body heat seemed to flow through her shirt to

her bare skin. For a moment Meg feared he might touch her, and the next, she wished he would.

They stared at each other, their gazes meeting, then blending and melting together. His arm drew back, and his hand gripped the edge of the table.

Her eyes drifted to his lips. They were soft and full, and she just bet he kissed with the same passion he exuded. She chastised herself for the thought. She needed to keep her mind on finding a doctor for the clinic.

"Think you'll ever practice again?"

"No. I've started a new life." The words rang through the small kitchen. His eyes flashed with conviction and his jaw tightened, accentuating the heart-shaped mole.

"That's too bad." Intuitively she knew Steve was a good doctor, and she wondered what had happened to make him not want to do what he was trained to do. Maybe he *was* burned out. Or just tired of big-city medicine.

He rolled the iced-tea glass between his palms.

"I'll bet you are a darn good doctor," she blurted. The man sitting across from her had just implied it took heart to be a good doctor. Meg sensed Steve cared deeply, and when she got this kind of feeling, she was never wrong.

The cold glass soaked the heat from his hot flesh. Sitting across from Meg Graham had made his hands warm and sweaty. With all the talk about being a doctor and whether he planned to go back to medicine, the top of Steve's head felt like it was about to blow off.

"I'm not a doctor anymore." Those words were his mantra now. And at times like this they felt right. He picked up the glass and drained it. Then he pushed the wooden chair back and stood.

She gave him a sincere look. "Sorry to hear that." Her brown, velvety eyes filled with compassion.

Meg's words soothed him for a moment. He did miss his old life, but it was better this way.

"I need to get back to the house. Thanks for the tea and the use of your phone." He crossed to the door. The screen squeaked as he pushed it open.

Steve heard her chair scoot against the linoleum, and he turned back. She picked up the empty glasses and made her way to the sink, her hips swaying.

A fiery blaze started in the pit of his stomach.

If he was in any mood to be attracted to a woman, it would be Meg Graham. She possessed a delicate yet strong face and a sensuous mouth. And her body...

His eyes stroked over her full, lush curves.

Indulging himself a moment longer, he let his gaze slide up slowly, admiring every tempting inch. Meg was sexy. Steve thought of soft skin and sweet scents. It would be easy to let his problems fade away, with her in his arms.

With no hesitation, he imagined Meg without a

stitch of clothing. He liked what his mind conjured up, and the need to get Meg into his arms rushed through him.

She faced him, her lips curled in an inviting smile. "Have you decided where you're going to sleep?"

The tightness in his jeans increased. "Uh…in my car."

"Oh, no!" Her chin tipped up, showing her smooth, curved throat.

His mouth went dry and his thoughts swirled with wonder. What would it be like to kiss her porcelain skin and let his lips trail down to the sweet indentation at the beginning of her throat?

"That's bound to be uncomfortable. There's not much room in the back seat of a BMW, is there?"

"I don't know." The answer hung in the air between them.

"Well, back seats aren't all…that comfortable." Meg's cheeks flushed. "Not that I've been in the back seat of a car in years…."

Hot summer nights and Meg!

His body pulsed with the need to hold her in his arms. What the heck was he thinking about? He needed to keep his mind on his house, his new life.

"There aren't any motels close by. I want to start on the house repairs early tomorrow."

She leaned back, her right hand resting on the curve of her hip. "I have plenty of room right here, and it's next door. Why don't you stay with me?"

"What?" The offer sent a powerful sensual message to his brain. He and Meg together!

"My guest room is warm and clean, and it sure is a heck of a lot more roomy than—"

"That would be too much trouble." Good sense told him he needed to stay away from Meg, yet he knew *that* wasn't going to be easy.

"You won't be any trouble. I'm hardly ever home. And you don't have to worry about the rent. Around Jackson we barter a lot. I get bread, pies, even eggs for my services."

"I don't have anything to trade."

She smiled again and his heart beat faster. She was so pretty and sweet...so sincere.

"Sure you do. Everyone has something someone else wants."

Right now all he wanted from Meg was to hold her and kiss her pleasing lips.

"While you're working on the Lemon House maybe you can help me with a few odd jobs around here."

Her practical suggestion made Steve realize a soft, clean bed *would* be better than the back seat of his car. And he'd have access to a working bathroom. Yet he'd vowed to stay far away from anyone who had anything to do with medicine. Meg Graham, he'd learned already, was a dedicated doctor.

"Come on. You'll be doing me a favor." Her soft, feminine voice feathered against his reserve like smooth silk. With eyes closed, Meg took a deep breath, and the action melted a thin layer of ice surrounding his heart. For a moment, Steve forgot where they were.

"How would I be doing you a favor?" he asked.

She opened her eyes and crinkled her nose. "The house repairs."

"I don't have any experience with what you're talking about."

"It doesn't matter. I'm a patient woman. I'll get you a key." She went to the teddy bear cookie jar on the counter and took off its baseball cap lid. "This fits both the front and back doors." She crossed the kitchen and held out the extra key.

He knew he shouldn't, but he let his fingers uncurl. She placed the warm metal in his palm, and he stared at the key. Meg could talk a blind man into buying eyeglasses.

If he did a few odd jobs around her place, he wouldn't be obligated in any way. And in a few days, he'd be only her neighbor, not her houseguest.

As if to negate his last thought she laughed. "It's official. You're my roommate. And once you get the Lemon House livable, you won't have far to move."

Steve thought about giving back the key, but she'd crossed to the sink.

"Go ahead and bring your stuff in," Meg nonchalantly called over her shoulder. "I only have one bathroom, so we'll have to share." She turned on the water, which pumped from the faucet full blast.

She hummed a familiar tune and her hips swayed to the melody.

Steve forced himself to stop gazing at those sensual undulations. If he was going to live with this mesmerizing woman for a few days, he had to draw a line. He made his way to the door and stepped out into the September night, wondering if he was in his right mind, accepting her invitation.

A mixture of emotions coursed through his veins. Sure, it would be convenient living just up the road from his house. But common sense told him he shouldn't let himself get any closer to Meg.

She sat on the couch and wondered if her earlier prediction was coming true. Maybe she *was* going off the deep end. Why in the world had she asked Steve Hartly to stay at her house? She'd never done anything like this in her life. But an uncanny feeling told her everything would be okay. She could trust Steve.

And she couldn't let him stay in his car, or worse, the Lemon House. She gulped and forced herself to think realistically. With Steve Hartly on staff, she could keep her clinic open. And she might be able to get some much-needed sleep. The last thought wreaked havoc with her rationale. If anything, Steve's presence in the house would preclude her sleeping.

Meg imagined Steve's fingers tracing against her skin, his body warmth enveloping her.

With a jolt she stood. What was wrong with her? She wasn't about to be attracted to another man uncommitted to his medical career. The experience with Andy had been enough for one lifetime.

Oh, for goodness' sake, Meg. Get a grip. You just met the guy and already you're comparing him to Andy.

She was acting silly. She was tired and worried about her patients and the clinic. Meg sank down again and groaned. Steve Hartly created havoc within her. What in the world would he be able to do when he was living in her house? She rubbed her eyes.

This kind of thinking had to stop. Getting involved with Steve physically wasn't going to help the situation—it could only hurt it. She had to convince the man to work at the clinic. The insurance company meant business with that letter, and she wasn't going to let her clinic close.

She tapped her bottom lip with her finger. Steve had been adamant about not practicing, but she only needed his help for maybe three months at the most. Just until she could get another doctor to move out to Jackson. And what was so terrible about rescuing him from that awful house next door?

The thought of anyone living in the Lemon House made her stomach knot. Why in the world would he buy a place like that?

She heard the screen door squeak open and shut. Her gaze darted up. Carrying one suitcase, Steve made his way through the kitchen to the living room.

"Can I help you bring in the rest of your bags?" Meg sprang off the couch, hoping to stop her heart from pounding so hard.

He lifted the bag a little. "This is it." He'd taken off his jacket and his forearm muscles rippled.

"Your room's on the right. Bath's the next door," Meg announced, and plopped on the couch again. Trying to seem unruffled with her new houseguest was hard work.

"Thanks." He tramped down the hall and found the guest room.

Meg watched his every step.

"If you don't mind, I'll take a shower, then hit the sack," he said over his shoulder. He placed his bag against the wall and flipped on the light. He scrubbed a hand through his hair and looked around.

"There are extra towels in the cupboard under the sink. Help yourself," Meg called. Steve moved out of her sight, and she stared at the carpet. From the gentle rustle, she knew he was taking off his shirt.

"Hope I'm not keeping you from anything." His words brought her chin up, and she gazed at the man standing in the hallway. His chest was bare, his right shoulder braced against the wooden doorjamb.

Meg tried to keep her eyes off her new neighbor's torso but found it impossible. Hard muscles etched an almost perfect physique. A fine matting of curly hair enhanced his chiseled chest.

She consciously closed her eyes. Maybe she was asleep, and Steve Hartly, standing in her hallway half-naked, was a sadistic dream her subconscious had conjured up.

Opening her eyes, she shook her head. Nope! There he stood in all his sexy glory. The first man to stand in her hallway looking like *that*, ever!

She drew in a breath and tried to relax. "Make yourself at home. If you need anything, just look around." She stood and prayed her legs would hold her.

"Thanks." The sensual sound of his voice was all Meg needed to propel her into the kitchen—as far away from Steve Hartly as she could physically get.

Chapter Four

The whoosh of water told Steve that Meg was up and getting ready for another hectic day. He'd had many hurried days in the Houston ER. Days when there wasn't enough time to even think clearly. Yet his work had been very fulfilling.

Steve made his way out of bed to the window. The pale gray morning was slipping the bonds of night, and the beginning of a Texas sunrise splashed across the sky.

Not far away the Lemon House sat in all its run-down glory. Steve shook his head. He was determined to get the place in shape and livable.

He stepped back to the bed and straightened the twisted covers. He'd thought the dreams troubling him would go away when he left Houston. But early this morning, when he'd found himself soaked in cold sweat and the sheet wrapped around his legs, he knew the move to Jackson hadn't helped at all.

The scent of Meg's perfume trailed down the hall and under the door, jarring him fully awake. Her fragrance reminded him of how beautiful she was. He raked fingers through his hair, then picked his clothes off the floor.

Moments later he padded out to the living room, hoping she hadn't left the house yet. He couldn't help himself; the need to see her again overwhelmed any other emotion. Lights were on in the kitchen, and he caught a glimpse of Meg as she crossed from the table to the counter.

Steve stopped in the kitchen doorway. Meg's shiny hair was tousled and she looked sleepy and warm. She was wearing jeans and a pale blue T-shirt. The softness of the shirt outlined her delicate shoulders and hugged her full breasts. A tiny red logo stretched across the supple curve of her bottom. His glance traced down to her bare feet. A slash of pink nail polish caught his eye before his gaze drifted up again.

The rich fragrance of coffee filled the air. Sniffing, he enjoyed the homey smell. "Good morning," he said, managing to keep his tone of voice neutral.

She met his gaze with a welcoming smile. Her face was bare of any makeup and she looked natural and pretty. "I thought I heard you. How about some coffee?"

"Sounds good." His body loosened a little. He

couldn't stop staring at her. He hadn't been with a woman in the gray, quiet morning for a long time. And standing in the doorway of the kitchen studying Meg caused him to feel, for a split second, alive and at peace with himself.

Meg turned back to the coffeepot and checked it. Steve remained in the doorway, and she felt his eyes on her. She tried not to enjoy the idea that he might be admiring her as she pulled two cups down from the cabinet.

Suddenly she yawned as she placed the mugs on the counter. Early this morning Steve's voice had woken her. At first she'd sat straight up in bed, her heart pounding but then she'd remembered he was in the next room. She'd fallen back against the pillow, her heart still thumping.

As she listened, he'd moaned a little and called out in a husky, sleep-ridden voice. She couldn't decipher anything he said; the only thing she knew for sure was that his voice was filled with torment.

"Coffee smells good," he said from the doorway.

She glanced over her shoulder and motioned him into the room. "Sleep well?"

"Yeah." He remained where he stood, his body filling much of the space. "How about yourself?"

She nodded despite the fact she hadn't been able to go back to sleep after his nightmare. All she could do was lie in the dark and think...about him.

She wanted to question him now, but knew she needed to mind her own business at six o'clock in the morning. Besides, after last night, she knew *that* kind of conversation would be much too intimate, and she was afraid he'd bolt. She needed to keep emotionally distant from him, for the clinic's sake.

She placed the mugs on the table and poured coffee into them. He found a chair and sat. "Thanks."

Smiling, she took a seat with the glass coffeepot still in her hand. "I bet you take it black."

He nodded.

"So do I. Learned to drink coffee that way in med school." She set the glass pot on the table.

"Yeah, me, too."

She lifted her mug to her lips and took a sip. "Good. Hot, though."

He reached across the table and outlined the name embossed on the mug. "Jim? A boyfriend?"

She smiled. "Hardly. It's my dad's. Mom gave it to me after I graduated from med school, before she moved to Galveston. It's about the only thing I have of his. I drink my coffee from it every day. Kind of a ritual. He's the reason I went into medicine. Whenever I feel like I can't go on, I think of my dad."

"He's gone?"

"Yes." She brought the coffee to her lips again, trying not to give in to the memories. She didn't want to talk about her father right now.

"You must miss him."

Her chest ached with the statement and she knew she'd better change the subject. "Remember pulling thirty-six-hour shifts in med school and drinking this stuff by the gallon?'' Meg rubbed her fingers against the blue porcelain, hoping to crush the tiny hurt starting in her heart.

"I don't miss those days, but it sounds like you're still working just as hard."

"Sometimes. It comes in cycles. There are days when I'm so busy I need to be three people, then it slows down enough so I can catch my breath." Meg smiled wryly.

"That sounds like a tough way to live and work."

"How are you going to make a living here in Jackson?"

Steve shrugged. "I've saved enough money for two years. By then I'll figure out something."

So he really *wasn't* planning on practicing. Frustrated and confused, Meg picked up the coffeepot and reached back to place it on the heating element. Pyrex glass connected with the tile countertop, a loud crack sounded and coffee splattered everywhere.

"Oh, heavens, what a mess." Embarrassed, she stood, pushed back her chair and stepped toward the sink. A shard of glass pierced her bare foot, causing a jolt of pain. "Ouch," she yelped. The wound was deep in the fleshy part of her foot.

Before she could reach the chair, Steve hastened to her side. "Take it easy," he said gently. He helped her sit, then knelt in front of her.

"Well, that was pretty darned stupid."

"Let me see," he demanded with confidence, while picking up her foot and cradling her heel in his palm.

Meg looked down again and closed her eyes. Silly how the sight of her own blood was making her light-headed.

Steve carefully prodded around the gash, and Meg winced. "You did a number on your foot." He glanced around the kitchen. "Paper towels?"

Biting her bottom lip to fight the pain, she nodded toward the sink.

He pulled over a chair and placed her foot on the seat, then quickly retrieved the roll of paper towels and pulled a few off, pressing them against her foot. Steve inspected the damage with steely eyes. "You need some stitches. I'll drive you to the hospital."

"Jackson's hospital closed a few months ago. Don't worry, I'll stitch it myself."

"Not a chance. I'll do it."

Fiery determination grew in his gaze, and she could easily imagine him taking charge in any hospital ER.

He grabbed her hand and placed it on her foot. "Hold these against the wound for a minute."

She let her fingers be guided as her face warmed.

"Where're your supplies?"

"In the hall closet. Leather satchel on the bottom shelf. There's a suture tray, antiseptic." She kept everything she needed for emergencies in the bag, never expecting she'd be the patient.

He was back in a matter of seconds, concerned and determined. She'd seen the expression many times with other doctors she admired. The reaction was an unknown *something* that kicked into gear and made the physician a true healer.

Pulling the paper towels away, he shook his head. "You really sliced it. But once it's stitched up, you shouldn't have any trouble walking. You'll just have to be careful." He fumbled through the kit. "Forceps?" He glanced up, frowning a little.

"Give me the bag and I'll hand you what you need."

He placed it on her lap. "Good thinking. It'll be faster working together."

She found some small forceps and passed them to him. Expertly, he dealt with the wound.

"You okay, Meg?"

She nodded, and he went on with his work, occasionally rubbing her foot and ankle.

He reapplied the toweling to the wound. "Your heart must be going a mile a minute."

The rest of her blood rushed to her cheeks. Her heart pounded harder. "I've never been stitched before."

"You'll only have a faint scar." He glanced up again, concern on his face. "Sure you're okay?"

She tried to give him a smile. His confidence calmed her. Steve Hartly was a darned good physician—her intuition hadn't been wrong. She handed him the antiseptic, then a syringe.

"Ready?" he asked.

"You'll be fast, and I can take it."

Their gazes tangled together in the intimacy of helping each other. Meg stared down at her lap. She was being silly. She needed Steve Hartly to be a doctor and nothing else. Squeezing her hands into tight fists, she tried to get her mind off her attraction for him.

Every few moments he took the time to rub her ankle reassuringly. In what seemed like a matter of seconds, it was over. Steve was good, fast and gentle.

He swabbed the now closed wound with antiseptic, then stood. "Better stay off it for a while. It'll probably be pretty sore."

"I can't. I've got house calls, patients to see—"

"Never slow down, do you?" He took the bag and set it on the counter, then gave her a stern look.

"People depend on me." She stood, trying to balance most of her weight on her good foot. "I'll just clean up this mess." She wobbled, almost falling.

His arm slid around her waist to steady her, and she fell against his chest. Her stomach fluttered, then cartwheeled up to her throat. His body warmth assaulted her reserve and made her dizzier than she'd felt a few moments before.

"I don't need any more accidents. I'll sweep up." A tiny wrinkle formed between his brows.

"No, I'll do it." She tried to stand alone, pulling

away, working to balance her weight. Still unsteady, she fell against him again.

His arms wrapped around her. "Better not. There's glass all over the floor."

Before she could take another deep breath, he'd cradled her in his strong arms. The subtle scent of his aftershave made her feel helpless. Unable to protest, she laced her arms around his neck.

His boots crushed scattered glass as he carried her across the kitchen to the living room. "Feeling all right?"

His deep voice rippled through her body.

"Sure, I'll be just fine," she answered quickly, wishing he would put her down. A mixture of attraction and embarrassment washed over her as she enjoyed the physical contact with him. He held her so effortlessly, making her feel like a damsel in distress. To her chagrin, his muscles tensed and she actually felt even more helpless. "Please, I'll be okay." He placed her on the couch.

"You like being in control, don't you?"

She glanced up at him. His expression was stern, his eyes dark. "Well, yes, I like knowing what's going to happen."

"Most of us do." His arched gaze clung to hers and invisible sparks snapped around them. "I'll clean up the mess in there. You rest for a few minutes. Doctor's orders."

"I thought you weren't practicing anymore, Dr.

Hartly.'' She had to say it. He was too good a doctor to fall by the wayside.

His eyes lost the dark glimmer she found so attractive and a hard, protective sheen replaced it. Tension deepened the lines on his face. Without a word, he pivoted away from her and walked back to the kitchen.

Steve swept up the glass, then walked outside, taking the back porch steps in one stride. Intense rays of yellow sunshine had swallowed up the early-morning grayness. He kicked at the wiry buffalo grass edging the driveway. With autumn on its way, the verdant turf was beginning to turn to thatchlike straw.

A cold chill that had slithered over him like a sidewinder a few minutes ago was still with him. Twice already, in just two days, he'd broken his pledge not to practice medicine.

He walked down the driveway to his car, leaned against it and studied the Lemon House and then Meg's. They were so different. Meg had obviously taken care of her home. By contrast, the Lemon House needed someone's time and effort, some loving concern.

Steve groaned and rubbed his face with his right hand. He had a lot of hard, time-consuming labor in front of him. He was looking forward to the diversion. Maybe with the work he wouldn't think so much about Meg and Houston. He wanted nothing to do with either one.

He shook his head. The part about Meg wasn't true. What he didn't want in his life was what Meg lived for—practicing medicine. Her enthusiasm for her profession could never be dampened. And being around her would only remind him of what had happened in the Houston hospital emergency room. The face of the woman, nine months pregnant, had seared itself into his memory. And rightly so.

He stared at the pure blue sky. Many hopes and dreams had been shattered that night in the ER. The aching in his chest increased, and he tried to lose himself in the pain.

Taking care of Meg's foot had proved that the struggle to keep out of medicine wasn't going to be easy. As soon as he'd seen the distress on her face, the physician in him had clicked on like a light on an automatic timer.

I became a doctor again in a matter of seconds.

The face of the young woman's husband materialized in Steve's mind. Questions filtered into his tortured thoughts. How many lives had been changed that night? How much pain had the loss caused?

Everyone had been supportive except Steve's father. Shaking his head he reminded himself to face reality and remember his promise. He was finished with medicine. Hadn't his dad, the best doctor in Houston, given him that same directive? Sure, Howard Hartly had never said anything to him about what had happened at the hospital, but his silence had been enough of a message.

Steve heard the screen door slam, and he shifted his gaze from the gravel driveway to Meg. She hobbled down the path in sandals, a bandage covering her foot and a smile blazing across her face.

She looked so genuine, so exquisite in the warm Texas sunlight that the sight actually made his throat ache. Her beauty forced Steve to turn his head and gaze at the distant horizon.

It would be better for both of them if they didn't live so close, and he didn't find her so darned attractive. He steeled himself and turned his gaze back to her. She smiled again, the dimples in her cheeks growing deep and sexy. His chest tightened.

His constant awareness of her nearness when they were in the house had yet to wear off. Hoping to dispel any yearnings, he closed his eyes. When he opened them, his resolve had grown strong again.

"Hey, thanks for cleaning up the mess I made. Sorry you didn't even get a decent cup of coffee." Meg came up beside him and leaned against the front fender of the BMW. Her foot throbbed, but otherwise she felt fine. She was determined to solve the clinic's problem right now.

"No big deal." Not bothering to look up, Steve scraped his tan boot against the dusty ground.

"Cal get here yet?"

"No." His voice was low and raspy.

"Don't worry, he's dependable. When you see him, would you tell him to be sure Donna makes her appointment this week? Sometimes she forgets."

He nodded.

Meg glanced at his profile. His lips were pressed together as if he was thinking about something terribly important, but his expression was noncommittal.

"Donna gets so busy with the ranch. I worry about her." She combed her hair with her fingers. "You know how it feels. You've been there."

He nodded again and drew a heavy line in the dirt with the toe of his boot.

"Steve, listen. I have this fantastic idea." She waited for him to look at her.

His gaze remained fixed on the ground.

She continued anyway. "I need help. Actually, what I really need is a full-time doctor at the clinic. But for now I could use an extra hand. Why don't you be that person? You can take a small part of my caseload—all afternoon appointments so you can work on the Lemon House in the mornings."

Not bothering to look up, he kicked at a small pebble.

"I'll even let you pick which patients you want. No house calls. I'll take all the evening calls."

She stared at him. His expression was so stern. She placed a hand on his shoulder.

"Steve?"

He looked at her and deep confusion flared in his eyes.

"What's wrong?"

"That part of my life is over."

"But it's a wonderful opportunity. Trust me, you'll come to really care about the people who live here." She had to persist for the clinic's sake.

More confusion narrowed his eyes. "No. It doesn't work that way for me."

"You might change your—"

"I won't." His voice was low, full of determination. "I'll never practice again."

"Steve..." She waited for him to go on, to take back what he'd said, but he just looked off into the distance, his face grim.

"I just thought...you said you...I can see you're a wonderful doctor."

He turned, facing her. He looked so resolute, yet she wanted to understand why he felt the way he did about something she loved so much.

"How can you give up such a gift?"

He shook his head. "I lost a woman and her baby because of the system you're fighting right now. After that I knew I needed to make some changes in my life."

"I'm sorry." She stopped, wanting to touch him, to soothe his obvious distress.

"I know I'll never practice again. I had no intention of even clipping a hangnail until I came here," he said.

Urgently wanting to understand him, she tried again to get through to him. "But people need us, Steve. I feel stressed sometimes, but...I don't understand." She reached out to him, pleading with him to explain the unexplainable. "It's wonderful being a small-town doctor. I think you'd really like it."

He stared at her for a long moment, then leaned toward her and brought her into his arms. With surprising ease, he positioned his mouth over hers and kissed her with a rising passion

The sudden move startled her for a moment, and a gasp escaped from her lips. His mouth was as soft as she'd imagined it, his embrace strong and enticing. She let her arms circle around him, her hands clasping him to her. Powerful muscles tensed as she kissed him back.

She didn't feel like a stranger in his arms. In fact, she felt practiced and confident kissing him. His breath mixed with her own, and she enjoyed the very closeness of him against her body. His mouth on hers made her think of crazy things. Like slipping her hand against his chest and tangling her fingers in his thick hair there, or guiding him back to the house and straight to her bedroom.

The insane idea scared her, but she didn't mind. Rather, fear mixed with pure need seemed to enhance and heighten all the senses in her body. She didn't care that Steve Hartly was completely and positively wrong for her in every way. She kissed him with all she had, refusing to harbor any negative thoughts.

Too soon he pulled away, leaving her lips bare and wanting. She prayed he would draw her back into his arms and kiss her again before reason took over and she ran into the house—but he didn't.

Confusion swept across his face. Without a word, he stepped back and then walked down the gravel road toward his house. He crossed his yard, climbed the steps and disappeared.

Meg's heart was still thumping against her chest. She swallowed hard. Steve made her feel womanly and out of control all at the same time. She drew her fingers over her mouth, then clenched her hand, trying to dispel the uneasiness she felt inside.

Why had she returned his kiss with such fervor? She needed him to help her, not kiss her. If she could get him to practice medicine again, he could save her clinic. She wanted to keep everything aboveboard—shove her physical needs out of the way.

Hoping to clear her mind, she breathed in the rich, thick morning air. Even in her sexual haze and confusion she knew one thing.

She wanted to understand Steve Hartly.

From his living room, Steve saw Meg standing in the same place he'd left her a few moments ago.

He'd expected her to slap his face and stomp away when he'd kissed her. But Meg Graham hadn't reacted as he'd predicted.

Why in the hell did I kiss her?

The question stung him. He knew the answer. He wanted to keep her at a distance and he'd thought a kiss would do the trick. Maybe she'd even throw him out of her house and never speak to him again.

He hadn't expected her to kiss him back. And the baffled look in her eyes when he broke their embrace had nearly knocked him to his knees, reminding him that he wanted to kiss her for other reasons, too. Like feeling the softness of her mouth against his and tasting her warmth.

The pulsing in his groin chafed against his jeans. Thank heavens he still had a slight grasp of reality.

Why start something that couldn't be finished? Obviously, Meg wasn't the type of woman who went in for one-night stands. And he knew he couldn't leave her after one night.

Steve stared out the broken window. Meg was still standing in the driveway. The morning light danced in her hair.

Mercy, she was a beautiful woman.

Steve acknowledged another fact. It was going to be incredibly difficult to keep from kissing her again.

Chapter Five

Meg twisted the key in the ignition and turned off the engine of her car. An involuntary sigh fell from her lips as she leaned back against the seat. Her eyes burned and her head was pounding.

She'd received another letter from the insurance company this afternoon, reminding her of their demands and deadline.

After making twenty phone calls and not finding even one doctor who was willing to move to Jackson, she'd called a friend of a friend in Houston and asked about Steve. As she'd expected, his credentials were impeccable. Dr. Steve Hartly was well thought of at the hospital—the best of the best.

She was now determined to talk to him on a professional level and convince him he had to work with her. But to complicate matters, she couldn't deny she'd been thinking about him and the kiss they'd shared.

Three days had passed since they'd kissed, but to Meg, it felt like three seconds. Every time she thought of Steve, sexual electricity shot through her body as if she were hooked up to a battery charger.

And if that wasn't enough, every evening when she got home, he insisted on examining her foot. They'd somehow eased into an informal, almost impersonal way of behaving with each other. Neither had mentioned their kiss.

She opened the car door, and butterflies invaded her stomach. There was no way she could halt the sensual thoughts holding her mind and body prisoner.

Another sigh escaped. She had to get herself under control if she was going to allow him to stay at the house. More importantly, she needed to capture her runaway feelings so she could talk him into helping her with the clinic.

I need lots of luck in both departments!

She heard herself laugh. At least she was still thinking straight and keeping a sense of humor. Steve had been emphatic about not practicing, but she might be able to change his mind. She had to— there were no other options right now. But after the kiss, not thinking about him romantically all day long was almost impossible.

And then there are the nights.

For the past few evenings, she dreamed about

Steve and his strong body, warm and masculine, lying next to hers. Dreams that caused her to reach out in her sleep to embrace him.

Dreams that disappeared the minute she opened her eyes.

The crunch of gravel as she stepped onto the familiar driveway drew her back to reality.

A soft September sunset surrounded her with shades of orange and pink. The hot, muggy summer had been brutal, what with all the extra work. She stretched, took a deep breath and enjoyed the saucy breeze of fall.

Meg's gaze shifted to the Lemon House. The black BMW was parked in the dirt driveway. A pile of debris sat to one side of the newly manicured front yard. The dull pounding of a hammer echoed across the space. Steve had probably been working most of the day. Rebuilding the Lemon House seemed to relax him.

With him close by, she patted her hair and bent down to check it in the sideview mirror. It wasn't until she thought about putting on some lipstick and going over to say hello that she sighed resignedly.

She didn't need to worry about lipstick. And she certainly didn't need to walk any more than she had to. She glanced down at her foot. Cutting the top of her tennis shoe off to give the bandage more room had helped. The injury was healing fast because of the care Steve gave her. But because she was on her feet all day, the sutured gash throbbed constantly.

Her gaze traveled to his house again. The hammering had stopped. She could hear Alan Jackson's latest country hit. The new windows were wide open.

Meg forced her eyes away and slammed her car door. Her mind conjured up an image of Steve, standing in his living room, shirt off, jeans slung low, beads of perspiration forming a glowing sheen. With a hammer clenched in his hand, the muscles in his arms and back would cord beneath his tanned skin.

Her heart thumped up into her throat, and she licked her lips, now suddenly dry.

Hearing his front door slam, she looked up. Steve walked down the three steps of the porch. His unbuttoned shirt lifted and floated as he strode toward her. A light matting of hair accented his strong chest, then narrowed to bisect his flat stomach.

He was heading right to her. Meg tried to take a step toward her house but couldn't move. Turning back to the car door, she found her lab coat was caught. She yanked at the material. It was held tight. Grabbing the door handle, she lifted it.

She'd locked the car! In a rush she scrambled for her car keys, but dropped her purse, and the contents hit the gravel.

"Good gracious," she muttered, trying to reach some of the fallen objects.

"Pardon me?" Steve stood not three feet away.

Her cheeks flushed hot as she glanced up. Unidentifiable white flecks dusted his hair, and dirt streaked his sweaty face. Her eyes traveled quickly downward. Without the soft breeze, his shirttail hung down, yet his dark chest hair peeked through and beckoned to her, urging her fingers to tangle in it.

"I said 'good gracious.'" She tried to sound nonchalant as she turned and gave her coat an extra hard tug. The last button stopped the material from sliding through the door. Facing him, she detected a smile playing at the corners of his mouth.

"Always stand around in the middle of your driveway?" He bent down to pick up the jumble of objects that had been in her purse.

"No...well, I mean, I'm caught." She tugged again to show him. "The button on my lab coat...I locked the car and the keys..." She pointed to the ring he'd just retrieved from the ground.

The keys jingled as he shook them. "Here you go." The sun dipped closer to the horizon and bathed them in more sunset colors. "Nice afternoon," he said.

"I need my keys." She put out her hand.

"Which one is it?"

"The oval one next to the chain."

Steve moved closer, the heat from his hard body mingling with her own. He smelled good, like work—manly and sexy. The combination caused a sudden jolt in her stomach.

He unlocked the door and easily released her.

Then he picked up the rest of her belongings and put them back in her purse. "Not sure what goes where—"

"It doesn't matter, thank you."

Steve offered her the bag and she took it. A moment later, as she walked toward the house, she found him beside her.

"How's your foot today?" He opened the screen door and motioned for her to go ahead.

"It's fine. Still aches a little, but nothing I can't handle." She limped into the kitchen and flipped on the overhead light.

"Did you elevate it today?" He stepped to the sink and washed his hands.

"It's fine." Her foot wasn't the problem. It was her pounding heart and wet palms that really worried her. She placed her purse on the counter and turned back to him. In the bright kitchen light she could see that his handsome face was etched with fatigue and grime. "How's the Lemon House coming?"

"Good. Cal came by and brought some of the plumbing fixtures I needed."

"Great."

"His wife make her appointment?"

"Yes. Thanks for reminding Cal again."

Steve stood in front of the refrigerator. "Want something to drink?"

"Thank you." She went over to the kitchen table and pulled out a chair, wincing as she sat down.

Now that she was home and relaxed, she felt the throbbing in her foot even more.

He turned around. "Are you in pain?"

"A little. I'll live."

Before she could say another word, he was beside her, untying the lace on her shoe and pulling it off her foot. His closeness chased away any idea of an argument. "I'll change the dressing." His warm touch was comforting and almost made her cry, it felt so good. He left to get her medical bag, and when he returned, he leaned down to take off the bandage. Checking the wound, he clucked his tongue. "You ought to stay off your feet as much as you can."

"Steve, I can't. I'm too busy."

"You need to elevate your foot on a chair when you're at your desk. When the stitches are ready to come out, I'll remove them."

"I can do that."

He glanced up. "I want to do it."

His statement danced between them like the last notes of a song.

"Good weather for fixing up your house." She used the benign words as a shield. Being so close was unnerving.

"Yeah, great." He cleaned the wound and bandaged her foot, then placed it on a chair. "Now I'll get us something to drink."

Meg cursed herself for missing his caring touch, and wondered what in the world was going on inside her. A hand on her ankle shouldn't make her breath come faster and her stomach tighten.

She raised her gaze and watched him as he stood in front of the open refrigerator and searched for iced tea. His jeans were dirty and the sharp creases gone. The denim fitted over his rounded bottom perfectly and made him more attractive. His legs, even though they were covered, still looked muscled and strong.

Before she could drop her gaze, he turned.

Heat traveled from the back of her neck into her cheeks.

Goodness, he caught me checking him out!

"Did, uh, did you…" she stammered. "Did… how's the work going on the house?"

"You asked me that already."

More blistering heat singed her face.

"I'm enjoying the work," he said. "It's nice to watch the house taking shape. The accomplishment feels good."

"Like practicing medicine?" She took a chance and brought up the subject. Maybe the solitude of working on the house had helped him rethink his decision.

He sat across from her. "I'm good at a lot of things."

The comment, although innocuous, reminded her of their kiss. "Well, you do kiss very—" Now why had she blurted that?

"I wasn't talking about the other morning." Steve

laughed and arched his brow. "But tell me, how do I kiss?"

Meg knew he was teasing her now. "Just fine. Like you've had a lot of practice."

"I had a lot of practice when I was teenager. Not so much after I left school. How about you?"

She giggled. "I didn't. I was somewhat of a wallflower in high school." She needed to change *this* topic fast. "The new windows you installed look great."

"Yeah, thanks to Cal's help." He paused and took a sip of iced tea. "The man is handy."

"He's helped me, too. I've known him and Donna ever since I was a kid."

"Is that why you came back to Jackson—because of the people you know?"

"Yes, and I love Jackson. I wanted to practice in a small town. Why not my own?"

"Nice talking to someone who knows what they want." Steve's expression turned pensive.

"From the time I was a little girl, I wanted to be a doctor. Had an entire doll hospital before I was ten. I'd cut off their legs and sew them back on." She laughed at the memories. "Of course, that's not my philosophy now." She laughed again.

"You're a natural. You make all the right choices."

"Not always."

Steve choked on the iced tea he'd been sipping.

"You? Not go the right way? I find that hard to believe."

"Oh, I've made mistakes. In med school I fell in love with someone who was totally wrong for me. Found out a week before the wedding."

"A *week* before the wedding?" He shook his head in amazement. "That would certainly throw you."

"It did, in a very big way, believe me." Meg nibbled on her bottom lip. Even though it'd been years, the unhappy memories were still fresh in her mind. "Have you ever been married?"

"No, never found the time or the right woman. Now, when I hear about so many marriages breaking up, well, I'm glad."

Knowing Steve hadn't been legally attached to someone made her relax a little. "Yeah, I'm glad I found out when I did, although it was tough at the time."

"Did the louse cheat on you?" He leaned forward, studying her.

"No. Worse. He thought he was going to talk me into practicing with him in Dallas instead of in a small town when I graduated. What he was really interested in was having two large incomes instead of one. He wanted to incorporate, belong to the country club, run with the movers and shakers. Unfortunately, he didn't bother to tell me any of this."

"You never talked about it before the engagement?"

"At first he went along with me and my own dream of working together. I found out about his real plans from his aunt, for goodness' sake. When I told him I didn't intend to have a showy practice in Dallas, he got angry. Told me I'd never be happy out here."

"He's a fool. And you must have been hurt." Steve's dark, compassionate gaze enfolded her.

She felt her stomach plummet again. He was the first man she'd told about her hurt. "That's not the half of it. It took me a long time to get my confidence back and not think of myself as just a moneymaking machine." She'd had such strong hopes when she'd accepted Andy's engagement ring. Dreams of a family, the perfect relationship, of working together. Losing it all had haunted and hurt her.

Meg sighed and looked around the small kitchen. She was happy in Jackson. She loved her work, the clinic, the people. At times she was lonely, but she was doing all right.

When she brought her gaze back to Steve, he was still studying her. "I proved him wrong. I'm happy now, and it was for the best. He wasn't for me. I was pretty naïve about life back then."

"Weren't we all?"

"I guess." She brought her fingertips up to her jaw and rubbed. Her face had grown tight from talking about Andy.

"Tired?"

"Not as much as last week. This week hasn't been too bad."

"Calm before the storm?"

"I hope not. Ever have weeks when you were so busy you thought the top of your head might fly off from too many problems and thoughts swirling around in there?" She tapped the top of her head with a fist.

A sneeze caught her by surprise, and she quickly covered her mouth.

"God bless."

"Thank you," she said with a sniff. The last thing she needed was a cold.

Steve's lips drew into a smile. "I enjoyed those hectic times. At night when I couldn't get to sleep, I'd think of every person I'd helped, and the satisfaction was pretty unbelievable."

An evening breeze curled through the screen door and stirred the air in the room. The smell of burning leaves enveloped them for a moment. The scent reminded her about Jackson's Halloween and Thanksgiving celebrations, pumpkins and holiday dinners with her cousin James Dean, his wife, Kate, and the kids.

Years ago Meg had wanted her own family and traditions. Now she was happy with what she had.

"I've told you my story. Now you tell me yours. Why did you go into medicine?" She took another chance asking such a question. Steve seemed relaxed tonight, and she wanted to know all about him, uncover what he'd hidden.

He drew in a breath. "Because that's what my family does. My father, my uncles, cousins—all are doctors in one place or another. I heard about what a great doctor I was going to be from the time I was five."

Meg imagined Steve as a little boy being pressured into a mold he wasn't sure he fitted, and her heart ached for him. "It must have been a tough act to follow. I'm the only one in my family who even has a college education."

"It's not that I didn't want to be a doctor. I did. I worked hard for it."

"But to have to follow in so many family footsteps, everyone expecting you—"

"Hey, I had it great. Look around. There's a lot of people worse off."

"Quitting must have been difficult."

He remained silent.

Maybe she'd said too much. She held her breath and waited.

He stared at her for a long moment. "The other day..." He paused and took a ragged breath. "I shouldn't have reacted the way I did. And the kiss—"

"I shouldn't have pushed you." Meg still didn't understand him, but she wanted to. She wasn't sure how she'd feel if she were in Steve's position, so she didn't want to criticize him for his actions. Medicine was a tough field and a lot of people in it had problems.

And she wished with all her heart she could eliminate the hurt she heard in his voice and saw on his face.

A slow drip from the faucet plunking into the stainless-steel sink seemed to echo as the silence stretched out between them. Her heart beat at twice the speed and she stared at the wall. "Doctors have limits," Meg said almost breathlessly, the blood pounding in her head. "We're not perfect, by any means."

Steve nodded, and more confusion filled his gaze.

Meg's throat ached for him. "We're under a lot of stress." Wanting to make a connection, she placed her hand over his.

"A woman came into the ER with preeclampsia. She was full term, in the throes of labor. She'd never seen a physician until that night because the family couldn't afford insurance. I did what I could...but it wasn't enough."

Meg found no words to reply. His face was pale. She knew with every fiber of her being that Steve cared a lot. Maybe that was what had made him quit. Steve Hartly cared too much.

She fought the urge to bring her fingertips to his cheek and stroke his skin—in comfort. Silently their gazes locked and held, understanding forming an instant bond between them.

Until, too quickly, Steve pushed back from the

table and stood, his eyes stormy. "Got to get back to work," he announced abruptly, then, just as quickly, left.

Meg thought about following him, but didn't. She was paralyzed with a deep compassion. She knew Steve better now, understood in some ways how he felt, and that knowledge scared the living daylights out of her.

Chapter Six

A shrill ringing woke Steve. He forced his eyes open. Darkness encased the bedroom. He glanced over at the curtainless window. A group of stars twinkled and glimmered in the black velvet sky. He kicked at the tangled covers around his legs. The telephone rang twice more and then stopped in mid-ring.

Meg's voice, a hushed whisper, traveled under the door, and his eyes opened wider. He sat up and swung his legs over the side of the bed. Yawning, he read the small clock.

Three-thirty.

He'd only been asleep a few hours. After talking with Meg in the kitchen, he'd gone back to his house. He'd needed the space. Hours later, after Meg had turned out the lights, he'd crossed the yards and climbed the steps. But when he went to bed, he found it impossible to sleep. Thoughts of Meg and their conversation rolled around in his mind.

She was the first person he'd ever talked to about the tragedy. Steve had valued his confidence. He never talked about the medical system's failures. But after losing the woman and her baby, he felt burned out and guilty for not fighting the insurance companies for charging so much. But Meg, with her honesty and genuine concern, had opened his heart a little.

The sound of running water told him she'd moved from the phone to the bathroom. There was obviously an emergency. He stood, found his jeans and tugged them on. She was probably tired, and her sutured foot wouldn't make it any easier for her to get around. Maybe he could help Meg in some small way. Steve opened his bedroom door and looked down the hall. Light from the bathroom slipped under the door into the hallway.

Suddenly, the door opened and she stood framed in the soft glow. The sweater and jeans she wore fitted her perfectly. Her hair was mussed and looked as if she'd just climbed out of bed.

She shifted and more light radiated from behind her. Meg looked beautiful, so natural and inviting. Desire cascaded through him. He wanted to hold her tenderly and answer his own sexual needs.

He saw her breath catch when she noticed him.

Her eyes widened and her sensuous lips part in surprise. "Oh, you startled me."

"Didn't mean to."

"Sorry I woke you." She combed her hair with her fingers, making it all the more sexy.

"Is there an emergency?"

"New arrival for the McWalshes. She's overdue by two weeks, so it's not a bombshell."

The idea of delivering a baby at home made his gut tighten into a knot. "So you're meeting them at the hospital?"

"Gosh, no. It's too far away, and the McWalshes can't afford it. They don't have a dime of insurance. She'll be fine." They stood in the middle of the semidark hallway.

"Yeah. Insurance companies can ruin good medicine."

"Tell me about it. But delivering babies is the mainstay of my practice." Meg limped past him down the hall and into the living room.

"Your foot is still hurting, isn't it?" The worry he felt for Meg overshadowed any other concerns.

"A little. It'll be all right."

"I'll drive you." He blurted the words out so fast he couldn't change his mind.

Her head jerked up and she smiled at him. "That's okay. I'll be fine."

"I know, but I'd like to help you. I'll wait in the car. If I drive you, you won't use your foot as much.

Besides, you shouldn't be out there alone at night—"

"I do it all the time."

"Let's not argue. I'm up and I probably couldn't go back to sleep if I wanted to. Just let me get my shirt." He headed toward his room.

Sitting on the edge of the bed, he tied his shoes. He'd just shocked the heck out of himself by his offer. He hadn't intended to drive Meg anywhere, but when he saw her limping, something inside him had taken over. Rationally, he knew he needed to keep out of this situation, but Meg had a way of turning everything around.

As he shrugged into his shirt, he wondered why he'd given in so easily against his resolve. By the time he finished buttoning his shirt, reality had filtered in and he knew the reason.

Last night.

He swallowed hard. His confession about what had happened in Houston had relaxed him a little. Meg hadn't criticized or tried to counsel him—just touched his hand gently. She was such a genuine person it was hard to keep his thinking straight. But he had to. Meg was a doctor first and foremost, and he wasn't anymore.

He crossed the room to the dresser and shoved his wallet into his back pocket. He'd drive her tonight, but from now on, he'd work hard at keeping his distance.

* * *

Meg forced herself to concentrate. She took her medical bag from the closet and checked the supplies. Steve's offer had astonished her. She'd thought the last thing the man would want to do was go with her to deliver a baby.

But she wasn't about to argue with him. The company would be nice. Texas country roads could be very lonely at three in the morning.

And it's one step closer to convincing him to practice again.

She mentally slapped the thought away. Manipulation and deceit weren't qualities she wanted to hone. He'd been darn nice to offer to take her to the McWalshes'.

"Ready?" His steady tone brought her out of her reverie.

"Sure. I'd hate for the baby to come without me. Although the parents could probably deliver the little critter better than I can. This one's their sixth."

"Old hands." He took her medical bag.

They drove in almost absolute silence. The only words spoken were directions she offered occasionally. The quiet surrounded them, and it felt nice just being with Steve.

Meg studied him in the dim light of the dashboard. Even in the middle of the night, he looked handsome. But his good looks weren't what intrigued her. Steve Hartly was a true enigma—the depths of his heart and soul going way beyond what she was used to in the men she had been involved with.

Andy had been all-surface, and so transparent in the end.

When she'd first met Steve, she thought he might turn out to be pretentious, but he wasn't. What little she'd learned about his personality seemed down-to-earth. Andy didn't have it in him to talk the way Steve did. Her ex-fiancé would never consider what was in his heart as a part of his medical practice. Medicine to Andy was prestige, money and getting ahead.

The heart-shaped mole on the right side of Steve's face was barely visible in the dim vehicle. She wondered if he'd been born with it, or if it had suddenly surfaced and marked him when he was a teenager and starting to think about romance and girls.

Her eyes drifted to his mouth. His lips were so soft. She remembered how they'd felt against her own—open and demanding, with warmth and need for her.

She shifted her gaze away from him. She didn't need to be thinking this way. She'd already let herself go too far and that scared her. Her total concentration should be on her work, not on how it had felt to kiss him.

To distract herself, she tried to recall how much she'd loved Andy at one time, but the memory evaded her. In the silence of the early, velvety morning, all she could remember was the way Steve had touched his lips to hers and how she'd responded. Her pulse had never skyrocketed or her body shivered that way when Andy had kissed her or made love to her.

Her gaze drifted to Steve's lips again. She thought of how they'd closed over hers with a mixture of tenderness and manliness she now craved. Meg wondered what kissing him again would be like. What if his lips traveled beyond her mouth, traced down her throat to her breasts?

Just as if she'd wished it, his tongue darted out to touch his bottom lip. She trembled and a little sigh escaped her lips.

"Cold?" His gaze found hers, and he smiled.

"A little. I'm more tired than I realized. Let's hope this won't be a long labor."

He switched on the car's heater, then reached over and patted her leg. The heat from his hand penetrated her jeans. She suppressed a moan. His touch was as comforting as she remembered.

"Are we almost there?"

"Um-hmm," she mumbled, afraid to open her mouth and let out the next sensual sigh that was threatening.

Meg turned her head and leaned her forehead against the cool glass of the passenger window. She prayed her heartbeat would drop back to normal. If her thoughts didn't slow down, she'd be in big trouble.

* * *

Jason McWalsh took three-and-a-half hours to come into the world, and Steve had waited in the car the entire time. Meg opened the BMW door carefully and stared at the man behind the leather-encased steering wheel. He'd fallen asleep. His head was tipped back against the tan seat, and his chestnut hair fell over his forehead, while his mouth was relaxed and slightly ajar.

He looked like the little boy he'd told her about last night. Butterflies assaulted her stomach. Even though she was tired, she hated to wake him.

"Steve," she whispered.

His eyes opened slowly, blinking as he turned toward the passenger side. "Is the baby all right?"

"Couldn't be cuter. Mother and son are doing beautifully," she said, climbing into the car next to him. She leaned against the soft leather and sighed.

"No problems?"

"None. Smooth delivery."

The corners of Steve's mouth curved up in a smile.

"I need to shower and change, then I'll come back in an hour or so." She fastened her seat belt and inhaled deeply, exhausted but satisfied.

"No time for a nap?" he asked as he started the car and pulled out onto the road.

"Afraid not. Thanks for waiting for me."

"Not a problem. I'll make you a cup of instant coffee when we get back to the house." Yawning, he steered the car with his left hand, stretched his right arm over the back of her seat.

His warm fingers trailed across her shoulder before they came to rest on the soft leather. Heavens, the man could do miraculous things to her heartbeat.

"A cup of steaming-hot coffee." She joined in his yawn and rolled her head, lifting her shoulders. "That would be ambrosia. There's something about bringing a new life into the world. You know, if I hadn't become a general practitioner, I think I'd have gone into obstetrics."

She nestled deeper in the butter-soft seat, then twisted toward him, leaning her back against the door. "I was going to ask you to come in, but I didn't think..." She stopped herself from saying anything else. The morning had gone too well.

"You're right. I wouldn't have. That part of my life is over. I'm ready to start something new."

The comfortable look was gone from his face, and a hard, blank stare replaced it. She didn't understand him, but she felt compassion for what he was going through.

Meg massaged her bottom lip with the tip of her finger. She fought the urge to share with him details of this morning. As a rural doctor she'd been cut off from colleagues—people she could relate to and who knew how she felt.

Her nose itched. She rubbed it, then sneezed.

"You're not getting sick, are you?" He glanced over at her.

"I hope not. I don't have the time." She sniffed, and another sneeze caught her by surprise.

"Throat sore?"

She swallowed in response, then shook her head. She'd been too busy to notice she didn't feel well.

"Fever?" The heel of his free hand pressed against her forehead.

"I don't think so."

"You're burning up."

His hand felt cool and soothing. The man was so compassionate, so caring. "I'll be fine. Drive with both hands. You're making me nervous."

His hand clamped back on the steering wheel, and he stared straight ahead. "We'll be home in a few minutes. Then I want you to go straight to bed. All the extra work's caught up with you."

"There's no way I can go to bed," she whispered, and slumped against the seat. The adrenaline that had pumped through her body earlier this morning drained out, and she became a rag doll.

Steve guided Meg out of his car and into the house. Taking her bag from her limp, hot fingers, he placed it on the kitchen table, his arm still around her waist. He could feel the heat from her fiery skin through her sweater. Without missing a step, he walked her from the kitchen through the living room to her bedroom. He led her to the bed and helped her sit down.

Kneeling at her feet, he untied her shoelaces. "Meg?"

She looked down at him, her gaze glassy and tired. "I'm fine," she croaked, her eyes only half-open. "I've got to get going."

"You're not going anywhere. Probably been incubating this virus for weeks. You've got a fever." He pulled her shoes off and tugged at her socks. He checked her stitches and rubbed her ankles.

She nodded. "Tired."

"At least you admit it. You're going to bed." He stood, reached down and grabbed the hem of her sweater, ready to pull it over her head.

"I can't stay home," she rasped as she tried to push his hands away. She glanced up at him.

Her hair was a mass of sexy twists and tangles, her face flushed. His entire body pounded with a fierce attraction for her, but he forced himself to step back. "You have to rest. You're exhausted and sick. I'm going to help you get undressed and into bed."

"I'm too busy. I'll be fine with a shower." She tipped her chin up again and stared at him, her eyes becoming more glazed with each breath.

"You've got to rest."

"I can't. Patients, the new baby. Three house calls today."

"Sorry, doctor's orders. To bed with you. Where's your nightgown?"

"In the closet, but I'm not putting it on." She struggled to get up, but fell against the pillow.

Steve went to her closet and found a soft white cotton gown. Just touching the material set his heart to hammering at a quicker pace. He turned back to her. "Here's your nightgown. Can you get into it by yourself?"

"I'm not staying home," she answered. But when she sat up and tried to grab for her gown, she fell against the pillow again. Her face grew more flushed, and a small moan came from her lips.

"Okay, that's it. Time for beddy-bye."

She nodded, her eyes closed. He was glad he'd driven her to the McWalshes' and was here for her now. The next step was to get her out of her clothes and into bed.

Just the thought of undressing Meg made him hesitate. He took a deep breath, reminding himself he was a doctor and had seen many female patients unclothed.

Meg's not just any female, Hartly.

That thought agitated him, yet he was determined to make her rest. He cupped her shoulders and helped her sit up. She groaned quietly.

He clutched her soft sweater by its hem and stripped it away from her body. Her white satin bra glimmered in the dawn sunlight streaming through the window. Her swelling breasts peeked over the silky fabric and rose with each breath. His mouth went dry.

Swallowing hard, he reached around behind her and undid the two small hooks. Her full breasts tumbled out of the lacy cups. His fingertips tingled at the thought of touching them, and he held his breath for a moment in an effort at self-control.

To push the unwanted feelings away, he quickly slipped the gown over her head. The soft cotton fell to her shoulders and then down to her waist. It touched places he ached to caress. He guided her arms into the sleeves as the pulsing in his groin increased and pressed tight against his jeans.

Steve silently scolded himself for his unprofessional behavior.

You shouldn't be reacting, Hartly.

He shook her gently. "Meg, can you get your jeans off?" He wanted very much to strip them away, to help her, to pamper her, to see the mystery of her, but he needed to step back.

Her eyes fluttered open and a silly grin spread across her face. "What?"

"Your nightgown's partially on. Can you handle the rest?"

She glanced down, then looked back at him, her eyes wide but not focused. "Yes."

"I'll make you some hot tea. If you're not undressed and ready for bed when I come back, I'll have to do it myself."

She stared up at him and then nodded. He left to go to the kitchen. After putting on the kettle, he searched for tea. Sometimes old remedies worked just as well as any modern medicine.

When the kettle whistled, he made tea in Meg's

favorite blue cup, her father's, and started back to her room. He hoped she had the strength to pull off her jeans. If not, he'd have to take them off, temptation or not.

Her clothes lay in a heap on the floor next to the bed, and he breathed a sigh of relief. She nestled on top of the covers, the smooth cotton gown barely covering her bottom. Her legs, golden and tantalizing, curved against the blanket.

Steve placed the steaming mug on the nightstand. She'd probably been fighting off the flu for days, running on nervous energy. All the work and practically no sleep had caught up with her. He slipped her gown down to her knees and tried to avoid touching her hot skin. Desire rose to the pit of his stomach, and he chastised himself again. If he allowed it, the longing would rampage through his body and negate every rational thought.

"I want you to drink this. But first you need to get under the covers."

She tried to sit up. "Doctor, I've got to go to work."

Doctor! His muscles tightened. Steve shook off the feeling for Meg's sake.

"No. You aren't going to work." He tenderly pushed her back against the pillow. He stroked her forehead and she sighed. Meg needed him now. He couldn't worry about himself.

Steve lifted her into his arms and pulled the blanket from under her. Automatically, Meg's arms wrapped around him, and she rested her cheek against his chest.

God, there's something so wonderful about this woman. The thought tore through him as he placed her against the crisp, white sheet, then pulled the covers up.

Her eyes fluttered open again. "There's a new baby to check on…my appointments." She struggled to sit up, blinking again, surprised to be in bed. "How'd I get—"

"Don't worry about that now. You don't want to expose the McWalshes to what you have, do you?"

"But what about my other patients?" She shifted her gaze away from him.

The anguish and defeat in her tone stabbed into his heart. He'd felt the same way when he'd finally decided he couldn't practice anymore.

To prepare himself, he'd hidden the concern he felt for his patients so he could more easily withdraw from his profession. He'd become unapproachable to everyone, even his friends and family. His plan had worked well, but only to a degree. Sure, he could cut himself off from everything and everybody—but he couldn't sever his own memories, his own feelings.

He missed medicine, but he was satisfied with his decision and determined to go on with his life. Until a moment ago, when he'd witnessed Meg's reaction, and his heart and soul had filled with the need to be a doctor again for her.

He gazed at Meg. She was staring at him with wide eyes, her cheeks flushed from fever. Each day she grew more enticing, more beautiful. Just the sight of her rendered him speechless.

Steve thought about her dedication, her integrity, and his throat hurt and his eyes started to burn. Meg was a doctor who cared. He'd been that kind of a doctor until he couldn't take any more of the system and he'd decided to get out. And he wasn't going back.

Meg flung the covers from her legs and swung her feet to the floor. Her nightgown inched its way up her thighs. Her bare, silky skin made his breath catch in his throat.

Steve slapped his libido back down before he sat beside her, wrapping an arm around her shoulders. Grasping the blue mug, he brought it carefully to her lips. "Drink this."

She sipped the steaming liquid. "Good."

If she didn't stay in bed, she'd only make herself worse, and he'd feel terrible. He clucked his tongue in exasperation. There was no way he was going to let that happen. Yet he wasn't happy with what he had to do to prevent it.

"Tell you what." The sternness of his voice brought her gaze up to his. "If you get back in bed and rest for twenty-four hours, I'll take your patient load. But only for that long, and only if we can get somebody over here to take care of you."

"I'm fine—"

"Stop arguing. You don't always have to be superdoctor. You're sick. Happens all the time. You're not getting out of bed. And you need someone to stay with you. Whom can I call?"

"That's silly—"

"I'm not leaving till I know someone will be with you." Her expression turned serious.

"My cousin, James Dean Pruitt. He or his wife will come." Meg got in bed, and he tucked the blanket around her.

"Okay. What about house calls?"

"Call my receptionist, Sandie—the number's by the phone. She'll give you a list. Plus the new baby and Mrs. McWalsh."

His stomach sank and a metallic taste seeped into his mouth. He'd forgotten about checking on the newborn. Meg gazed at him, an anguished look on her own face.

"Steve, maybe this isn't such a good idea...." She slid the covers back.

Seeing her commitment and strength, he remembered the good things about practicing medicine. "I'll take care of everything," he said as he stood. "Get some rest so I can get back to work on the Lemon House." He started to the door.

"Steve," Meg whispered from her bed.

He turned at the sound of her voice. Her hair had fanned out against the pillow, and her eyes were now closed. Sick as she was, she was still lovely. "Yes, Meg?"

"Thank you."

Chapter Seven

Steve sat at Meg's desk. Neat stacks of paperwork covered the flat surface. The day had gone better than he'd expected. After calling her cousin and getting a promise that someone would be at Meg's house within the half hour, he'd driven back to the McWalshes'.

The newborn and mother were healthy. When he left the house, he actually felt as if he'd accomplished something. He spoke with Sandie at Meg's office, made the required house calls, then came back and dealt with patients. The last appointment of the day had been with Donna, Cal's wife.

Steve glanced around Meg's office.

What in the heck have I gotten myself into?

Weeks ago he'd decided he wasn't going to fight the medical bureaucracy anymore. That meant not practicing. And now he was right back in the thick of things. Sure, it was easy to diagnose a cold or prescribe a blood pressure medication for one day, when he wasn't burned out or overworked with insurance problems and patients who were fighting the system, too.

He looked around the office again, deciding the room reminded him of Meg. Nothing ostentatious about it or her. It was inviting. Steve stood and crossed to the pictures hanging on the wall.

One photo showed Meg standing by an ostrich, of all things. Another featured an older woman and Meg with a mortarboard on her head, a diploma in her hand and a smile to light up the night on her face. Obviously the day she'd graduated.

Another photograph showed Meg as a little girl sitting on the lap of a man in ranching garb. Her tiny face was tilted up and beaming with admiration, her arms wrapped possessively around his neck.

Steve took a step to the right, to examine a family group shot—a man who vaguely resembled Meg standing with a pretty woman, each holding a child. All of them looked about as happy as anyone could hope for. Maybe it was her cousin and his family.

His stomach tightened. He'd wanted a family at one time. Wanted it with all his heart. But during college and medical school, he'd been so worried about doing as well as his father had done that he hadn't taken time for any serious relationships.

When he'd returned to Houston, he'd dated plenty

of women. Finding a date as an up-and-coming doctor had been easy. The hard part was finding one he liked.

None of them was like Meg.

The realization didn't surprise him at all. Forcing his eyes away from the photos, Steve moved back to the desk, sat and picked up a pen. He had a few more insurance reports to write, then he'd be ready to go home and see if Meg was better.

This morning his offer to work at the clinic had proved something: that his feelings for Meg had progressed way beyond what he'd intended or was good for either of them.

He rolled the pen between his thumb and index finger. The best thing he could do was force himself to forget about the past few hours, the past few days. And put an end to his crazy feelings for her.

"Hey, Mego, feeling better?"

Meg opened her eyes and focused on her cousin, who sat in the chair next to her bed with a newspaper folded on his lap.

"Yes," she croaked. "Maybe...I guess I'm not going to die."

"You've been sleeping all day."

"All day! What time is it?"

"Five. Kate's out in the backyard with the kids. She made a casserole." He nodded toward the kitchen. "I baby-sat. Brought Charlie and Vanessa over a little while ago." A fatherly smile appeared on his face.

From the open bedroom window she could hear the children giggling in the backyard. Her fever was gone and she could actually think straight.

"You watched the kids all day?" she asked.

"Charlie and Vanessa about ran me ragged." James Dean rubbed his chin. "When's your *friend* coming back?"

She'd expected the inflection on the word *friend,* and she couldn't help but smile a little. "I'm much better. You can take Kate and the kids home."

"I'm worried about you."

"Twenty-four hour flu, that's all. I'll be back in the saddle tomorrow." She glanced down at her gown. "How'd I get into this?"

James Dean shook his head. "Don't look at me. And Kate said you were in bed sound asleep when she got here." His eyes widened and his eyebrows lifted almost to his hairline.

Meg's cheeks flushed with the memory of Steve undressing her.

Oh, for goodness' sake, girl, he's a doctor.

The thought didn't stop her pulse from racing.

"All kidding aside, who is this guy?" James Dean inched to the edge of the chair.

She was surprised it had taken her outspoken cousin as long as it had to get down to the business of finding out about Steve.

"He's my next-door neighbor."

"Sure. The only house close by is the Lemon House. We assumed it was somebody you met in Dallas, and well, you know. It's been a long time since you've even had a—"

"Let's not talk about *that*." She sat up in bed, and her head swam. Bringing her hands to her forehead, she pushed her palms against her eyes and fell back against the pillow. "Whoa, I'm not as well as I thought."

"Don't get your panties in a twist. So you met this guy in Dallas?"

"No. Steve's the doctor who helped Erin Waldron at the Sunshine."

His eyes grew wider. "He's living with you, isn't he?"

"Yes. Just *living* and working on the Lemon House. Nothing more."

"You let a stranger move in with you?"

"I'm trying to convince him to practice at the Jackson Clinic so I can keep my insurance. I've still got that to worry about." She felt her stomach knot at the thought of closing the clinic.

"Nothing else going on?"

She shook her head.

"Listen, Meg. I know how a person can get all riled up. Happened to me when I met Kate. You've got to take these things slow."

"I offered Steve my guest room. That's all. Believe me, there's nothing going on between us." But the memory of their kiss sprang into her thoughts, and though she tried to push the image away, Steve's handsome face and soft lips kept drifting into her mind.

Confused, she lay back on the pillow. She needed to convince Steve to practice with her, and not daydream about kissing him again.

"He's been at the clinic most of the day. Kate told me he called three or four times to check on you. Maybe he'll be the solution to the clinic problem."

The idea of Steve's working as a doctor again thrilled her. But the information that he'd called to see how she was troubled her. They needed to keep their relationship totally on a professional level. Besides, she didn't want Steve to worry about her.

"Steve's a great doctor, but he doesn't want to practice anymore."

"I'd put my money on you to talk anybody into anything. You didn't have any trouble talking me into helping Kate with her Lamaze."

Meg nodded. She did have a way of convincing people, but Steve's situation was different. "You and Kate were easy. You were madly in love with her. Steve's had rough times. I'm not sure I can be that persuasive."

"Just your luck."

"Whose luck?" Steve asked, his large frame filling the doorway.

When she saw him, Meg automatically sat up straighter and combed her hair with her fingers. After having a fever and rolling around in bed for hours, she knew she looked a fright.

"Mine. We were just talking."

Steve entered the room. James Dean stood, and Meg introduced them.

"Thanks for staying with her," Steve said, nodding toward Meg as the two shook hands.

"No problem. We're family." Her cousin eyed him warily.

She'd seen that look from James Dean many times, whenever he was acting protectively.

"It's good to have family who care." Steve shifted his weight.

"Meg! Meg!" Kate's anguished voice reached them through the window.

She sat up, her heart pumping. "What is it, Kate?"

"Charlie can't breathe."

Meg pushed back the covers and swung her feet to the floor, then sprinted across the room. Steve and James Dean followed her to the backyard. They found Charlie and knelt by his side. The little boy was wheezing. Kate and James Dean stood together, clutching Vanessa between them.

"Where's his inhaler?" Meg asked his parents.

"He said he lost it in the tall grass in the field," Kate cried.

"Oh no! I don't have one in the house," Meg stated, and looked at Steve. "We'd better drive to town."

"I'll try finding his inhaler," James Dean yelled as he ran toward the field.

Steve placed his left hand on the child's shoulder, his right against Charlie's spine. "Meg, calm down. I've seen plenty of asthmatics in the ER." He looked into the little boy's eyes. "Charlie," he said, his voice incredibly composed. "I'm Doc Steve. You're going to be all right. Just watch me breathe." The heel of his hand moved up and down the boy's spine.

The fear in Charlie's eyes didn't lessen, but he gazed at Steve and breathed slowly, evenly.

Steve continued stroking Charlie's back. "Charlie, keep watching me while I breathe." He kept pacing his breath, drawing the child's attention to his. "Easy, nice even breaths. Just relax." His hand continued to run the length of Charlie's back.

The little boy gasped, his breath raspy, his eyes still big, full of fear.

"Steve..." Meg began.

He held up his hand without losing eye contact with Charlie.

"Hey, big guy, breathe slowly, calmly. Watch me breathe. Take an even breath. That's good." A determined yet confident look graced Steve's face, and his tone was soothing, caring as he stroked the child's back.

Meg watched in wonder as Charlie slowly relaxed, his muscles loosening, the panic in his eyes fading.

"Breathe, Charlie, slowly."

Fifteen minutes later, the child was breathing normally, without rasping at all.

The group stood in the living room now, and James Dean thrust out his hand. "I can't thank you enough for helping my son," he declared with obvious emotion.

"It was no problem. I've had plenty of practice with kids in the ER." A distant look filled Steve's gaze.

Kate smiled weakly. "Thank you so much." She shifted Vanessa to her right hip. "We'd better get these kids home."

Meg's shoulders felt limp with fatigue. "Try to keep him calm," she said.

Kate and James Dean both nodded.

"No more excitement for tonight." Meg reached over and hugged Charlie. "Don't worry, you were just overexcited. You take it easy. You have another inhaler at home?"

The little boy nodded.

When her cousin and his family left, Meg plopped on the couch and sighed.

Steve sat down next to her. He reached over and pressed his palm against her forehead. "No fever. How do you feel?"

"Better. A little weak. You were great with Charlie. I don't like treating family. It's hard to detach."

"Isn't that the first rule in medical school? Only

treat strangers?'' He smiled and brought his arm
around her.

"Thank goodness you were here."

"Yeah," he said, his voice low and distant. The
muscles in his face tightened.

She put her hand on his forearm. "Are *you* okay
should be my first question."

"Yeah, I'm fine."

"Sure?" She brought her hand back to her lap,
her heart pumping.

He gestured toward the front door. "Nice family.
You're lucky to have them around."

"Since Daddy's gone and Mama moved, James
Dean's all I have left. We give each other advice
sometimes."

Steve nodded, but any hint of a smile was gone.

"Are you sure you're okay?" Meg pressed.

He turned to her, his gaze serious. "I promised
myself weeks ago I wouldn't practice, ever, and
now…"

Meg shifted a little so she could see him better.
She could smell his aftershave, see the start of dark
stubble, which accented the heart-shaped mole on
his chin. Her fingers tingled with the need to touch
it just once.

"Maybe you're not supposed to avoid medicine,"
she said softly. "Ever think of that?"

His jaw tightened more. "Meg, I was a good doctor. I loved it. It's just…the medical system is so
messed up. It really hurts people."

"You care. That's what counts. The night in my kitchen when you told me about needing a big heart to be a doctor...it's true...." Her voice broke with emotion.

"Even if I had the biggest heart in the world, I could not have saved that mother and her baby."

"But you can help other people who need you. Bring other babies into the world. Help women who—"

He held up his hand. The hurt and concern on his face were evident. "Medicine isn't for me. I'm really clear about my decision." He stood and gazed down at her. "I hope you understand."

She nodded as a lump formed in her throat. Maybe giving him more space to think and recover would help. With time, he might change his mind.

Steve took a deep breath, then turned and walked into the kitchen.

Meg decided to take a quick shower. She needed her own space right now to sort out feelings she didn't care to experience—strong, turbulent emotions she'd never felt before.

She took a deep breath and held it for a moment. She didn't want to face it, but she wondered if she was falling in love with Steve Hartly.

Steve stood in the bright kitchen. A moment ago he'd left Meg abruptly because he'd almost leaned over and kissed her. He shook his head and told himself to forget about caring for a woman who loved medicine so much.

"Damn," he rasped. He'd never felt this way about anyone. Was he falling in love with Meg Graham?

He shifted his gaze to the backyard, and the same emotions he'd experienced an hour ago welled up in him. A deep satisfaction had overwhelmed him when he'd helped the little boy. Being a part of medicine had always made him feel as if pure oxygen was coursing through his veins.

Steve shook his head. No, he couldn't step back into that dynamic world again. He'd made his decision and he needed to stand by it.

The rich blue of Meg's coffee cup sitting on the counter caught his eye. He picked it up and rubbed his finger around the handle. She'd said it was her father's—said her daddy had been the one to encourage her to practice medicine.

Steve had wanted to talk to his own father about the anguish he'd felt when he'd lost the woman and baby. But there had only been silence between them.

And then one night, when the memories overwhelmed him, he'd decided to leave medicine. Steve stared at the rich blue of the cup. He'd made his choice and he would never go back.

Meg turned up the volume on the small kitchen radio and two-stepped around the room. She felt so healthy.

Steve had taken over her practice for a few days so she could recuperate, and the rest she'd gotten had done the trick. She'd returned to the office with a burst of new energy. Plus, Steve had plowed through more insurance claims than she could have in a week.

Alan Jackson repeated the chorus to his latest song and Meg sang along, dancing back to the sink with an iced-tea glass in her hand.

She smiled.

Working at the Jackson Clinic had done her roommate some good, too. Her patients were raving about him. And he seemed to be smiling more. Yet, as soon as she'd felt well enough to go back into the office, he'd returned to the Lemon House.

There was only one negative with Steve helping her. It had played havoc with her resolve. With all her patients praising him, she was finding it more difficult to stay aloof. She'd caught herself staring at him many times and thinking about him all the time. Thank goodness the Lemon House would be finished soon. With Steve in his own place, there'd be less temptation.

With that positive thought, she two-stepped toward the refrigerator.

"Nice moves."

Steve's deep voice cut across the kitchen and Meg stopped dancing midswing. She turned to face him.

"Why, thanks. I was just practicing for tonight."

He was standing on her back porch, a grin gracing his face.

"It doesn't look like you need any practice at all." He opened the screen and walked into the kitchen. His dark eyes remained on her and her heart gave a little jump like it always did.

"A person can always improve her two-step."

"Is that what that was?" His approving gaze traveled over her body, and Meg enjoyed the attention.

"I'm practicing for the country-and-western dance tonight. Do you dance?"

"Not much."

"Every weekend the Sunshine turns into the Starshine Café. People come from miles around to visit and dance a little." Meg two-stepped over to the table.

"And you go?" His brow hitched up a little.

"Of course. It's a great way to connect with my patients. I learn more about them at the Starshine than I do in the office. And dancing relieves tension." Meg twirled to make her point.

"There's something to say for small-town medicine," Steve said.

"There sure is. Why don't you come with me?" She gripped the back of the chair she was standing next to. This would be a way for Steve to get to know her patients on a personal level, and he might find out that being a rural doctor was worth it.

"Nah, I'd better not."

"Why not? You've been working so hard on the

Lemon House. Besides, you're the talk of the town. My patients love you.''

"They do?"

"Sure they do."

Meg studied him for a moment. She wanted Steve to realize what a good doctor he was. Going to the local dance was a way for him to see how much his patients appreciated him. And he might even relax and have a little fun.

She rested her hand on her hip. "You're not one of those guys who's afraid of a little dancing, are you?" She allowed the smile that was threatening to appear.

"Of course not."

"Right! I know your type. Macho men don't dance, you don't like chick flicks, poetry bores—"

"Just to show you, I'll go. Besides, I'm all caught up around the Lemon House."

"Great!" Meg clapped her hands together and the noise jumped around the room. Why did she always act so goofy when she was around Steve?

"If I'd known I'd get that response, heck, I'd have said yes right away." He smiled again. "By the way, you look wonderful."

Meg's heart pounded harder. She glanced down at the simple dress she'd forgotten she was wearing. Heat rose to her cheeks and she nibbled on her bottom lip. Maybe going to the dance with Steve wasn't such a good idea, after all. She shifted her gaze back

to him. He was still smiling, his eyes full of anticipation.

There was no way she could take back her invitation. She'd just keep her feelings tied in a lasso
and not let go.

"And you said you couldn't dance," Meg called
over the throbbing beat of the fast-paced, country-
and-western tune.

Steve's heart slammed against his ribs. He managed a wink, then smiled at Meg. She grinned back.
For the last hour, they and thirty other Jackson residents had been two-stepping around the cleared
floor of the Sunshine Café.

"I never said I couldn't dance. You assumed it.
Actually, you dared me," Steve said.

She laughed and dipped her shoulder toward him
as they both swayed to the music. "Well, I have to
say you proved me wrong. You're good. I bet
you've done this before."

"Never." Steve was pleased he'd picked up the
dance steps so fast. In Houston, with his heavy
workload, there'd been no time for any recreation.
"This is fun."

"Now grab the lady and two-step to the left," the
instructor called over the jovial melody.

Steve seized Meg, his arm easily wrapping around
her waist. Mercy, life felt so good when she was
close. Meg fit perfectly against him.

"Now two-step back," the instructor called.

They moved together as if they'd been dancing with each other for decades.

"Wow, I'll have to start calling you Fred," Meg whispered in his ear, her breath fanning his skin.

His heart pumped harder and he gazed at her. "Fred?"

She leaned back in his arms a little and smiled her sexy grin. "*Fred Astaire.* You know, the dancing star in those old black-and-white musicals? You can really dance."

"It's my partner! You're making me look great."

"True." Meg's tongue darted out and touched her bottom lip, then disappeared.

Steve thought his knees might buckle and was thankful when the music ended. Meg must have felt the same attraction because she immediately stepped out of his embrace.

Her hand fluttered to her heart. "Wow, talk about a workout."

Steve knew he'd never seen a prettier woman. A soft country ballad started and someone dimmed the lights.

"A slow dance. I don't do those," Meg announced, and moved off the floor.

Steve followed her. Cal and Donna were sitting at a table by the front door.

"Hey! Y'all looked great out there," Cal said, and grinned. "You and Meg been dancing at the Lemon House?"

Steve shook his head.

"You two are the perfect couple," Donna said, and rubbed her large belly. "I wish I could two-step tonight, but Cal won't let me."

Meg was at Donna's side in an instant. "How are you feeling?"

"Like I'm ready to explode." Her hand crossed over her abdomen again.

"Are your ankles swollen?" Meg's expression changed to worry and she studied Donna. The woman was so conscientious.

"No. They're fine if I stay off my feet. I miss dancing with my man." Her arm landed on Cal's shoulder.

"Donna, after the baby comes you can dance all you want," Steve exclaimed.

The door to the café opened and Sue Waldron walked in. "Y'all should see the show outside. Shooting stars are painting the night sky."

"Oh, I love to look at stars," Meg said in a low voice.

"It's about time you stopped working." Without thinking, Steve took Meg's hand and ushered her out the door. A moment later they were standing on the sidewalk looking up at the velvety Texas sky. The air was crisp, with a hint of smoky promise in it. Steve inhaled deeply. He'd never had time to watch shooting stars, dance the two-step or spend time with a woman like Meg.

"Isn't it wonderful out here?" Meg asked.

"Yes. It is." Anywhere would be magnificent as long as Meg was by his side.

The sweet strings of another ballad swirled out from the café and found them. Meg did a little two-step toward him, then laughed and looked up.

"Did you have a good time?" she asked.

She was close enough that he could detect her body warmth and enjoy her scent. Meg always made him feel like he was on top of the world.

"I had a great time."

"Good. I read a study in a medical journal about dancing and what a great form of exercise it is. I recommend it for some patients who suffer from tension."

Tension.

Steve wasn't sure anything could get rid of the stress he was feeling at the moment. The only thing that might do that was kissing Meg.

He shifted his attention to the night sky. He had to get control of his thoughts. Kissing Meg could only cause problems for them.

"I'm always amazed at how many stars I can see on a night like this," Meg said.

He'd forgotten how dramatic a night sky was without interference from city lights.

"It's one of the prettiest sights in the world, isn't it?" she whispered.

Steve turned back to her. Meg was bathed in the muted light from the café and she was ravishing, her hair gleaming and her skin looking so soft. "It sure is."

The café door opened and Cal and Donna appeared. "Excuse us," Donna said, and then slipped her arm through Cal's. "We didn't mean to break in—"

"We were just looking at the sky."

"Is that what they're calling it now?" Cal asked, and Donna laughed, her fingers touching her lips. Then they started down the sidewalk to their pickup.

"Donna, don't forget your next appointment. And stay off your feet." Meg combed her hair with her fingers as her gaze followed them.

When the couple was out of sight, she turned back to Steve. "Guess we'll be the talk of the town."

"Are you always working?"

She nodded. "It goes with the territory. But I love what I do."

"Even with all the bureaucracy?"

"No, I don't like the paperwork or the rules. But I work around it. People like Cal and Donna are important. They aren't to blame for what the system has turned into."

"True." Meg had a way of putting things into perspective. Before he could stop himself, he draped an arm around her shoulders. To his surprise, she didn't pull away. Meg snuggled closer and leaned her head against his shoulder.

Together they gazed up at the sky, and the stars winked back at them.

"Oh, look at that shooting star! Isn't it beautiful?" Meg pointed and lifted her chin a little. "I'm going to make a wish."

She closed her eyes and took a deep breath as if she were about to blow out birthday candles.

God, she was beautiful and sexy and everything he wanted in a woman. How could he resist her?

Without another thought, he turned her to him. She opened her eyes. Steve leaned down and let his lips gently touch hers. They were warm and sweet. She opened for him and his tongue found her recesses.

Meg moaned and pressed against him. They continued to kiss, to enjoy each other.

Suddenly the door to the café opened and they were bathed in bright light and music.

"Oops, sorry folks."

The door closed but it was too late. Meg was out of his arms and Steve felt as if his heart had been ripped from his chest.

She stood five feet away, her eyes wide and her lips in a firm pout.

"Come back here," he demanded.

"That shouldn't have happened. We came here to dance."

"Kissing you feels better."

"Steve..." She lifted her arms a little, her palms up, frustration showing in her eyes.

"You can't tell me you didn't like kissing me."

"I liked it. That isn't the point. I just don't think

we should be kissing. We're sharing a house in a small town. I'm the local doctor...."

She had a good point. They didn't need to get involved. Her life was her practice and he wanted none of it.

"You're right. It won't happen again."

"I am and it won't?" Her expression had turned to pure surprise. She blinked and some of the astonishment melted. "I certainly didn't expect you to agree with me."

"We're going to be neighbors. It's best not to get involved. That can only complicate matters." Steve knew he had his work cut out for him. All he wanted to do was bring Meg back into his arms and kiss her senseless.

She crossed her arms. "You're right. We have to work at being neighbors without all this." She turned and walked back into the café.

Drenched in bright sunshine, Meg drove along the Texas highway. She turned up her favorite country song on the radio and let the wind dance through her hair. Then she glanced in the rearview mirror and her smile grew. She caught the flash of joy in her eyes. The warm, early fall breeze lifted the hair off her nape and played with her skin. Meg sniffed the air. Texas autumns were so inspiring.

Today another patient had stopped by to tell her what a great job Steve had done. That's when she'd decided to make a picnic dinner, invite him out to the lake and talk him into working at the clinic.

A bit of desperation tightened her spine, but she shook it off. She'd gotten another telephone call today from the insurance company reminding her how many days she had to find another doctor.

She had to take the chance. The town needed Steve. And besides, they'd managed to stay away from each other for the past few days. No kissing, not even a touch.

Despite her resolve, she sighed just thinking of the kiss they'd shared in front of the café the other night.

Meg shook her head. Steve had said it wouldn't happen again and he'd kept his word. She had to do what was best for the town. She'd talk Steve into working with her so Jackson Clinic would not close.

"I can't, but thanks for asking." Steve glanced at Meg, then brushed some plaster dust from his jeans.

"I've got everything ready. Just for an hour. Come on, Steve, you need a break."

"Well…" His resolve to put distance between himself and his temporary roommate began to melt.

Meg looked beautiful—almost mythical—standing on his porch with the cresting sun backlighting her brown hair.

"I won't take no for an answer." She perched a delicate hand on her hip and smiled again. "I owe you for your time at the clinic."

"Count it as rent." His pulse raced. She'd come over to the Lemon House with a grin on her face, excited about a picnic, and all he could think about was how he wanted to take her into his arms and kiss her again.

"It's just an hour out of your life."

"The repairs on the house aren't going as well as I expected." He nodded toward the living room. "Cal and I started the new drywall, but he had to stop."

Meg brushed a strand of hair from her face. "Why?"

"He said he can't come back for awhile. He doesn't want Donna saddled with any of the ranching chores. I agreed with him."

"Can you do some of the work yourself?"

"Some, but with drywall, you need two people at least."

"Well, you have to eat. I made some great food."

His stomach growled, but he was more hungry for Meg's lips against his than for any meal.

"You need a break," she insisted. "I'll pick you up in thirty minutes."

She smiled again, and Steve felt as if the breath had been knocked out of him. The last of his resistance slipped completely away. "What can I bring?"

"Not a thing. I've got a wonderful basket packed and there's no chance of rain."

The late-afternoon breeze picked up and ruffled

her silken hair. Her special scent floated over to him, a warm, woodsy perfume that was extremely distracting. He fought the urge to reach out and smooth her hair.

"You'll love the lake."

Her voice brought him back to reality. Meg wasn't picture-perfect, not at all. But her healthy good looks, combined with the way she moved, spoke and faced life head-on, made her the most beautiful woman he'd ever come in contact with. In his eyes, she was a flawless package.

Yet there was something more, and he knew it. It was the very essence of her he found delightful—the inner person. And he relished every moment with her. That was why he couldn't say no to her invitation.

"Great, I'll be ready."

Meg nodded, turned and walked down the steps and across the yard. The sexy sway of her hips, which she was so unaware of, made him gulp, and a sensual fire started to burn at the pit of his stomach, then blaze a path to his groin. He indulged himself and let his eyes follow her until she was out of sight.

Steve turned back to his work. He needed to fight his attraction for her. He'd go on the darned picnic but keep his feelings in check.

Chapter Eight

"You look great," Steve said, and glanced across the cotton blanket she'd spread out on the sand.

Meg's cheeks grew hot, and she cursed her reaction to his vague compliment. She drew in a deep breath and glanced at Crockett Lake. A light breeze fanned across them, making the late afternoon perfect for an outing. "Thank you."

"Lake's nice." His gaze traveled out to the horizon, and they watched the egrets swooping down to the nearly still water.

"This is really the best spot in the area. My family and I used to come out here all the time when I was a kid. During the summer, we'd swim all day."

"You and James Dean?" Steve positioned himself on his side, his dark brown eyes studying her.

"My parents when I was younger, friends as I got

older,'' she said easily. She liked talking to Steve. "How'd you spend your summers?''

"Went to the beaches in Galveston till I was twelve, then I worked in my dad's office processing insurance claims.''

"So that's how you got all my paperwork finished so fast.''

He nodded.

"Twelve's kind of young to be stuck in an office, though.''

"Yeah. But back then I would have done anything to please my father.'' His chest rose and fell in even cadence and he concentrated on the lake's horizon.

It was obvious he didn't want to dredge up memories. And she needed to keep the conversation light so he'd be in a good mood when she asked him to rethink her offer.

"Hey, are you thirsty?'' she asked, rising to her knees and making her way to the large wicker basket behind them. Digging past cloth napkins, knives and forks, she pulled out a bottle of wine.

"Looks like you brought enough food for an army.'' He took the wine and held it in both hands, examining the label. "Good year.''

She laughed easily. He was only being nice. She'd bought the white wine at the local grocery in town and there hadn't been much choice. "Thanks. A country special. It's chilled, so it should be fine.''

"Jackson's a great place.''

"What do you like about it?" Her heart beat hard. If he liked Jackson, that was a positive step.

"The people. Cal's been great and Donna even made me a pie and some cookies. Ran into James Dean at the hardware store and he invited me over for dinner. Waldrons came by yesterday and brought fresh milk from their cow." He turned the bottle around in his hands. "Good people, all of them."

She handed him the corkscrew she'd remembered to throw in the basket at the last minute. "Yes, they respect you."

He went to work on the wine, ignoring her last comment. She noticed calluses on his fingers. Suddenly she was thinking how their roughness might feel against her bare skin, on her waiting breasts, circling her—

"Meg," he said softly, holding up the open bottle. "Are you ready for me to pour?"

She glanced at his face. He'd been watching her. The satiny darkness of his eyes made swallowing difficult. Heat shot downward through her body. Shaking her head, she laughed with uncertainty. What in the world was wrong with her? Meg didn't need to think about her answer.

"I've got two real wineglasses...somewhere." She dug into the basket to distract herself.

"They're on the blanket."

She looked up. He pointed to two glasses sitting side by side, then inched closer. The corded muscles in his forearms moved under his tanned skin, the sprinkling of chestnut hair accenting them. To distract herself, she began to arrange the containers of food.

"Don't worry about the food now," Steve said.

He held her hand and guided her closer until they faced each other on the blanket, their bare knees almost touching. She could feel the heat radiating from his body, and her face warmed.

"Your hands are like ice." He rubbed her fingers.

She wanted to tell him they were always cold when she was nervous or unsure. "Cold hands, warm heart," she said, reciting the cliché quickly.

He laughed and handed her the glasses, poured a small amount of wine into each, then took one. She drank a sip of wine to steady her nerves.

"How is it?" he asked.

"Okay."

"Just okay?" He raised a brow. He sampled, still staring at her over the rim of his glass. "A subtle flavor, soft, beautiful." He smiled. "Not pretentious, sexy without knowing it."

She laughed nervously and took a bigger gulp of wine.

He raised his glass and drank in turn, never taking his eyes from her. "What do you think?"

Her heart was pounding, yet she managed a shrug. "I don't know much about wines."

His eyes blazed so torridly they seemed to melt the clothing from her body. "Wines are like people."

"How?"

"This wine reminds me of you."

Her heart skipped a beat, and her fingers grew more icy. The picnic was a very bad idea. Why hadn't she just asked him to come work for the clinic while they were back at the Lemon House?

After pushing himself off the blanket, he reached down for her hand. "Take a walk around the lake with me. Work up an appetite."

Maybe a walk would soothe her nerves. She stood on her own, facing him. "Aren't you hungry?"

"Not now. My mind's on something else." He seized her hand and laced their fingers together.

She wanted to argue with him but didn't. Heck, she wanted to do a lot of things. Like run away as fast as she could.

But somehow the warmth of his skin against hers took her reason away and splintered all her reservations.

"A walk would be nice. It's really pretty around the lake."

For a moment, Steve forgot *why* he'd suggested the walk. Then he looked at Meg and remembered.

Thrusting himself up from the blanket had been a way to stop the captivation he felt for her. But now it was obvious the quick move hadn't worked.

His body pulsed with need for her. Just a moment ago, he'd been picturing her naked, lying seductively against the blanket, her dark hair tumbling against her shoulders, her mounded breasts waiting for his touch.

The throbbing of his manhood increased. He shook his head, trying to escape from his lustful thoughts.

Hell, I don't know what I want anymore.

His gaze trailed back to Meg. The setting sun laced the sky with ribbons of yellow and pink, and the vision of her against the dancing light made his gut tighten. He fought the urge to pull her into his arms and cover her in kisses.

Meg can make me forget almost everything.

"It's lucky I remembered to put candles in the picnic basket," Meg said.

"Candles are good," he said. He squeezed her hand and her heart raced.

"Yeah, great idea. It'll be getting dark in awhile. But we still have time to check out the lake. You can't see it from here, but there's a cove about half a mile after the rocks. At the top, you'll get a great view of the whole area."

They walked close to the shore, where waves lapped against the soft sand. She pulled her hand away from his and quickened her pace. Maybe if she didn't touch Steve, the tight feeling in her stomach would go away. She laughed out loud at the hopeful thought.

"Something funny I missed?"

"It just feels wonderful to be here." She let her gaze follow another flock of egrets. Against the sun-swept sky, they looked like paper cutouts someone had thrown into the wind.

"Did you climb these rocks when you were a kid?" Steve asked as they looked at the craggy incline.

"A million times, at least," Meg called out, then sniffed the air. The mixture of water, fresh air and sand smelled exactly the same as when she was a child. She, James Dean and her parents had come out to Crockett Lake almost every weekend. That had been before her father's accident. She started up the rocks.

Her throat hurt and she bit her lip. Now wasn't the time to be thinking of her father and the past.

Steve and she reached the top together, and Meg straightened. She peered down to the rippling water.

"It seemed a lot higher when I was a kid," she said breathlessly, pushing her hair back from her face.

Steve stood beside her. "Everything does. I remember thinking my dad's office was like a giant maze when I was little, but as I grew up, it became just another doctor's office."

"Great view of the lake." Meg pointed to the sun-soaked horizon.

His gaze shifted to her. "This is nice, real nice." They stood together, a light breeze skimming their faces.

"Ready to start down the other side?" Meg asked after awhile.

Before Steve could answer, sultry laughter and soft moans reached them. Meg and Steve looked at each other.

"Did you hear that?" he asked.

They craned their necks and squinted toward the cove below. More laughter and moans were audible.

"Somebody's down there," Steve whispered, motioning below.

"Sounds like more than *one* somebody," Meg announced. She stepped forward, trying to see who was making the noise. Another provocative laugh climbed up the rocky terrain toward them, followed by a delicate gasp.

Steve glanced at Meg with a knowing look and she suddenly felt light-headed.

"There's a couple down beyond the rocks. I can barely see them." His voice came out thick and raspy.

He drew her close, nestling her against his chest. Now she could see two bodies, intertwined, lying on a dark blanket. The two forms looked like one in the dim light—connected and fluttering in an age-old dance. Another moan emphasized what they were doing.

"Obviously, they're busy. I wouldn't want to disturb them," he whispered against her ear, and tightened his hug.

Meg's nape grew hot. The feather touch of his masculine leg hair brushed against her and sent pinpoints of desire through her entire body. She realized how close they were standing, their naked thighs and calves touching.

A sensual cry drifted up, starting a rush of reaction at the pit of her stomach that spread throughout her body.

"Well…we can't walk…any farther." Her own voice was husky and low.

"I guess not." He studied her in the dimming light. "Are you blushing?"

"No, of course not," she retorted, hoping she could hide what she was thinking. "I've seen plenty of naked bodies."

He glanced back to the sand and drew her closer. "Yeah, naked bodies, but together like that?" He swallowed hard. "You're right, we'd better get out of here."

His fingers stroked her shoulder, and Meg's stomach churned with a million butterflies. She pulled away, turning from the sight below and lunging toward the path they'd come up.

Halfway down the rocky terrain, Steve caught up with her. "What's the hurry?"

"No sense in staying around." The words came out much too fast. She felt young and foolish.

They finished the climb and jumped the last two feet to the soft sand. Steve caught her by the hand. "You're embarrassed, aren't you?"

"No…yes…I don't know. It's the first time I've ever seen two people…" She let her words trail away, not knowing what to say.

"Making love." He finished the sentence for her as they started toward the blanket.

"Yes," she whispered, breathless from walking so fast. "But I wasn't embarrassed. It was, well..."

His hand landed on her shoulder. She refused to turn and face him as his fingers massaged the muscles. Touching both her shoulders, Steve brought her gently around.

They were only inches apart.

"If you aren't embarrassed, then what are you feeling?" His dark eyes questioned her.

Meg shook her head. She wanted Steve to kiss her—needed to make love to him.

"Well?"

His question ripped away any calm. Finally, she raised her head and looked at him. His eyes had gone sultry, and her knees felt as if they might collapse.

"I wasn't embarrassed. But seeing the couple made me think about us...the way we've kissed. What it made me feel."

His fingers tightened and gently rubbed her shoulders. "You were thinking about me and you, together?"

She nodded, wishing she was anywhere else except standing so close to Steve.

"Meg, why do you think you have to hide your feelings from me? There's nothing wrong with being attracted to each other."

"You felt the same way up on the rocks?" She

blurted out the question before she could stop herself.

He arched a brow, and his expression was enough of an answer.

Her tongue slid around her dry lips. "I've got the clinic to worry about. I don't have time for any involvement."

"You work too hard." His hands were still on her shoulders, his fingers rubbing in small circles. "Sometimes you seem a million miles away. And then, other times..." He moved even closer.

"Working hard is just part of me. Saving my clinic is, too."

"Yeah, and so is imagining you and me making love."

She drew in a ragged breath.

"I worry about you," he said, his voice low.

"Worry about me? Don't bother, I'm fine." She tilted her head a little, questioning his interest.

"Trying to save the world is tough work," he whispered.

She rolled her shoulders, hoping to disengage his hands, but they remained. "Sometimes...being the only doctor at the clinic...well, it's a lot of pressure."

"Ever wonder if it's worth it? Why do you stick it out?"

His questions hammered at her, and she let her gaze drift to the lake's horizon in an effort to cut him off. Pressure from the threat of losing her insurance and being forced to close the clinic *had* made her wonder if it was worth it.

But what was bothering her now was being so attracted to Steve. She'd come out to the lake to convince him to help her. Talking about making love wasn't going to help. The other night at the café they'd promised to keep their distance, to not kiss anymore, and she had to stand by that pledge. They needed a professional relationship, nothing more.

"Why do you work so hard? You can tell me. I'll understand." He stroked her bare arms.

Her gaze met Steve's. "The people in Jackson, they're good people. They need me and the clinic. My dad needed someone." Her hands clenched into fists. She turned her head, but his finger found her chin and drew it back.

"Tell me, Meg."

"Steve, it's difficult to talk about something I've tried so hard to forget."

He sucked in a deep breath and let his hands drop to his sides. "I can relate to that. I've tried to forget my life as a doctor. But it doesn't work. Memories will haunt you if you try too hard to push them away." Pausing, he blinked his eyes. "I think about that night in the ER all the time." He stopped and cleared his throat. "I don't like to see you hurting, that's all."

A knot formed in Meg's stomach. Why did Steve

have to be so concerned about her? It only made him more attractive.

"Meg." His voice was husky. "Giving up medicine was the hardest thing I've ever done. I'll never be the same."

She understood what he was saying. They were soul mates in a way, sharing deeply held beliefs about their profession.

"I guess what I'm trying to say is you shouldn't be so hard on yourself," he whispered.

She tipped up her chin and closed her eyes. It felt so good to talk to someone who understood how she was feeling. A hot tear traced a path from the corner of her eye down her cheek.

Steve's fingertip caught it. "Meg, you can't do it all. I know. I tried."

At his warm, sensitive touch, Meg opened her eyes. "My dad died senselessly in a ranching accident," she told him. "He needed a doctor. If there'd been one in Jackson, he'd still be alive. As a kid growing up without him, I wished every day that someone, anyone, would have been here to help him."

She stopped and tried to swallow over the lump in her throat. "I guess I turned that someone into me. That's why I work so hard and can't let my clinic go. I won't ever get over being that little girl who needed someone to help."

Steve slipped his arms around her trembling body and brought her close to his chest as if to soak up her pain. Meg relaxed and pressed against him, a soft moan escaping her lips. His hand went to her hair, and he stroked it, his fingers moving gently.

The closeness wafted his special scent to her and made her think of warm apple cider and butterscotch—soothing and comforting.

His chin rubbed against the top of her head. "Sometimes things happen we can't begin to understand."

She wished Steve hadn't broken down her carefully built walls of reserve, but he had. Her last rational thought convinced her she needed to kiss him.

Chapter Nine

In a swift, deft move, she tilted her head back and studied his eyes. The warm autumn air brushed across their bare skin, sweeping away doubts, filling her with hope.

Steve lifted his face to the sky for a moment. Meg studied the heart-shaped mole on his jaw. It was a part of him, like his love of medicine. She brought her finger to his birthmark and touched it.

Steve's chest expanded against her. He moaned and drew her closer. Without any thought to the immediate future, she let him place his lips against her own.

Whimpering, she arched to meet him. Her arms tightened, and his lips traveled to her throat, any restraint slipping away.

Again their lips touched and joined. Meg tried to

hold back the dark, primitive yearnings but found it utterly impossible. Curbing her desire was like trying to stop the tide.

She wanted to fall to the ground with Steve and answer his sharp, insistent need. Her hands moved to the back of his neck. She sighed and parted her lips. Their union deepened as his tongue tangled with hers.

All the tension slipped from her body as they continued their sensual exploration. She responded as if in her own dreams, fully a woman, with a bottomless passion.

He kissed her harder, more fervently, making her forget everything except the man who held her in his strong arms. His right hand drifted to her breast. Easing back, without releasing her lips, he slipped his hand under the soft T-shirt material.

"Oh, baby," he sighed. One finger slid beneath her bra, and he stroked devastating circles against her skin. Slowly, he edged his finger farther, and she arched up, murmuring her acceptance.

"Meg, I want you."

Steve's words startled her. Her fingers disengaged from his hair and braced against his chest. Her once-pliant body stiffened. Meg tried to push him away, but he wouldn't budge.

She'd been lost in his kisses and touch a moment ago, but his words brought her back to reality and what was really important. She should be focusing on the clinic. People were depending on her. Kissing

Steve, going any further, would only muddy the waters and distract her. She suddenly felt overwhelmed by this avalanche of conflicting emotions.

"We have to stop," she said evenly, and pushed harder against his chest.

"What's the matter?" Steve let her go, then stared down at her, his arms limp at his sides, confusion etched on his face.

The setting sun slid behind some clouds at the horizon's edge and the sunlight faded. Meg welcomed the shadows, hoping they would hide her bewilderment.

Quickly, she turned and started back to the blanket. She needed time to regain her composure, get her thoughts together.

"Meg?" Steve came up and fell into step beside her. She knew what he wanted to know—why she'd kissed him so passionately and then cut and run.

"I'm sorry. I—I wasn't thinking," she sputtered, and kept on walking.

His hand was on her shoulder and the pressure made her stop. She looked toward the safety of the blanket and wished she was already there. She sighed and turned to face him.

He opened his arms wide. "What in the world are you sorry about?" His gaze grew as dark as the shadowy lake.

"I don't know. You've got me so confused right—"

"Confused? You knew exactly what you

wanted." He nodded to where they'd stood together a few moments before.

"I know. That's the confusing part."

"I learned a long time ago that some things aren't explainable."

"I have to control my feelings when I'm around you." She studied him. His face was still ruddy with passion, his eyes torrid. Her hand flew to her own cheek and she rubbed it. The skin, sensitive from his whiskers, burned. "It's ridiculous, acting like this," she admitted. She should be talking to him about the clinic.

"Who was acting? If you can control what goes on between us when we're together, you have more strength than I do."

She studied his lips, remembering how they'd pressed against her throat and mouth. More burning need welled up inside her and she sighed.

"Steve, I never understood Andy. It wouldn't be fair for me to get involved with someone else I don't understand. You want to give up medicine, and I thrive on it. We shouldn't take this any further."

He looked at her carefully, digesting her statement. "Yeah, maybe you're right."

"I've got an early appointment tomorrow. We need to eat," she said. Forgetting what had happened a few moments ago was really the only course to take.

"Fine with me. You're the doctor." He shrugged, but waited for her to start toward their picnic site.

Meg lit the candles while she watched Steve stare out at the darkening lake. He looked so handsome.

The foolish thought made her clench her jaw. She still needed to convince him to help her rescue the clinic. She sighed deeply.

Steve glanced at her. "Are you okay?"

Meg had to ask him. He was too fine of a doctor not to help her.

"Steve, I talked to some people in Houston. You have an impeccable record. You're more than good at practicing medicine. People at the hospital said you did all you could for the woman and baby." She stretched out her hands. "No one could have saved them." She stopped a moment to compose herself, catch her breath. "Practice with me. I need you. If I don't find a doctor, a capable doctor, I'm going to lose the clinic."

He didn't say a word, just kept gazing at the candle's dancing flame.

"If you don't, Jackson's going to be right back where it was when my father died."

She was trembling but glad she'd finally said all she needed to say. He'd help her now; she knew he would. How in the world could he possibly say no?

"So that's what's behind all this." For a long moment his eyes raked over her, questioning, then swept toward the picnic and blanket. When his gaze came back to her, his mouth was set in a firm line.

"My patients told me you were wonderful."

"Quitting had nothing to do with my ability. I don't want to fight the system anymore."

"But the folks in Jackson need you."

"So back there was all a ploy to get me to change my mind?"

She stiffened and took a deep breath. "You actually think I kissed you for that reason?"

"Maybe. And seeing that couple. Part physical reaction, part manipulation."

She crossed her arms. "All physical, believe me. You just happened to be there and the moment seemed right. Nothing but an animal urge." She didn't wait for a comeback. "I want you to help, need you, but kissing you has nothing to do with the clinic, nothing at all." Her skin heated.

"Interesting." He pressed his lips together, then picked up his half-full glass of wine and drained it. Turning slowly, he faced her. "I have no intention of going back into medicine. I'm not going to practice again."

"Fine." Her heart pounded into her throat, hurt feelings taking over her entire body.

"I'll move tomorrow. The plumbing will be in and the Lemon House will be habitable now."

Meg nodded, numb with confusion. She couldn't explain what had happened. But she was glad there was a wedge between them. Now there was no way she could get involved with Steve Hartly.

Yet desperation tore through her. She cared for

him and wanted him to be happy. Obviously he had to work out his own problems.

Meg took a deep breath and squared her shoulders. Tomorrow she'd start her search again, and she'd find a doctor before it was too late.

Steve hammered his thumb instead of the nail, and a string of expletives flew around the empty, disassembled living room. He dropped the hammer to the bare floor, shook his left hand and danced in a circle, trying to alleviate the pain.

The drywall he'd been holding against the framing slipped, crashed against his shoulder, then fell to the floor with a bang.

"Unbelievable!" Steve rubbed his shoulder. At the rate he was going, he'd never finish the repairs on the house.

He sat on the floor and stared at the unfinished wall. A soft morning breeze swept through the room, cooled his sweaty skin and reminded him of Crockett Lake and Meg. It had been a week since he'd packed up his belongings and moved. But it seemed like years, and his gut ached with loneliness.

He still remembered the keen, aching need he'd felt when he'd kissed her during their picnic. Meg wasn't the kind of woman who could respond to a man unless her feelings were deep and true. But Steve knew it wouldn't be fair to get involved.

He couldn't expect Meg to commit to him when he had so many problems in his life. She needed him to keep the clinic open, but something inside him wouldn't let him move forward.

He silently cursed the way he felt, not understanding it. The people who lived in Jackson deserved good medical care. But even though he was concerned for them, he couldn't step beyond the boundaries he'd established so carefully around himself.

The sound of gravel crunching under tires caught his attention. It wasn't Meg. She'd left early this morning and it would be nightfall before she returned.

Steve stood and crossed to the open window. Turning into his driveway, kicking up dust, was a caravan of pickup trucks. In the first vehicle was Lou Bowden, owner of the hardware store where he'd been doing quite a bit of business. Behind was Sue Waldron with a man who looked to be her husband. Pulling up the rear were Cal and Donna.

Steve walked out into the rich morning sunshine and squinted.

"Hey, Doc," Cal said, and grinned as he bounded out of his ancient truck. The large man made his way to the passenger side, opened the door and helped out his very pregnant wife.

Donna grinned and nodded. "Hey, Doc. How's it going? I saw Meg just a little while ago." She turned and drew a picnic basket from the bench seat of the truck.

Steve's body tensed with just the mention of

Meg's name. "Cal. Donna. Come to run me off the place?"

"Hell, no. Come to help you out. It's Jackson's way. One man can't do all this work. Donna brought some fried chicken for lunch."

Donna crossed the small space and hugged Steve's waist. She was extremely graceful despite her pregnancy. "We all decided you needed some help. I've promised Cal I'll stay off my feet when I get home." She hugged him again and her grin grew larger. "Thank goodness we have Meg. Don't know what the town would do without her." Her hand rubbed over her large belly. "Don't worry, I'm taking the truck and heading back home. My sister's coming by to watch over me."

"Yeah, so I'm free till noon." Cal glanced at the others. "The rest can stay till the work's done."

The small knot of people nodded.

Sue Waldron held up a caulking gun. "I'm the best darn caulker in the county." She grabbed her husband's hand with her free one. "John showed me how the first month we were married. Practically built the entire ranch house myself."

"It was mighty nice of you to help my boy." John Waldron stepped forward, hand extended.

"Anyone would have done—"

"Nah, you go ahead and take the credit. Heard you could use some help. This Lemon House used to be a nice little place. With our sweat, we'll getcha fixed up."

Steve rubbed his chin with his thumb. In Houston he'd lived in solitude, with no sense of community. To him it had been just a big, sprawling city of concrete-and-steel buildings. His gaze slipped from face to face. These were nice people. People who cared a whole heck of a lot about other people's happiness.

"Cal's gonna ramrod us," Lou Bowden stated. "I brought supplies. Figure we can get this place at least livable by nightfall."

Steve swallowed hard. Yeah, these were real nice people who deserved the best.

Meg dried the last glass and put it in the cupboard. She sniffed the air and enjoyed the homey scents. Kate and James Dean's kitchen smelled of roast beef, mashed potatoes and carrots.

Her gaze came to rest on the calendar hanging on the far wall. An ostrich with huge eyes stared back at her. James Dean and Kate were happy running their ostrich ranch together.

Studying the calendar, Meg counted the days since she'd kissed Steve. The time since then had dragged by. One week ago tonight, she'd been in Steve's arms at the lake. Leaning against the counter, she stared at the numbers. They blurred in front of her eyes.

"Hey, thanks for doing the dishes," Kate said as she walked into the room and plopped down in a chair by the wooden kitchen table.

"There weren't very many. It's the least I could do for a home-cooked meal." Meg shifted her gaze from the wall and looked at James Dean's wife.

"Are you all right, Meg? You seem a little out of sorts."

"I'm probably just tired," Meg said, and hung the dish towel over the oven door. She checked her beeper. No calls, thank goodness. She moved to the table. "How's Charlie? Any more asthma attacks?"

Kate shook her head. "No. He's been pretending he's Doc Steve and practicing his breathing."

Somehow Meg managed a chuckle. "Steve's a good doctor."

Kate rested her forearms on the table and another grin graced her pretty face. "Have you talked him into helping you?"

"No." A tense feeling welled in Meg's stomach. She'd spent the past week fighting her mixed-up emotions and looking for another doctor.

"I really thought eventually Steve would work with you at the clinic. Talk around town is that he's great. Some of the older ladies..." Kate rolled her eyes. "No offense, but I wouldn't mind seeing a different face once in a while when I bring the kids to your office."

"Steve...he has to make up his own mind." Meg didn't want to go into details. Even this small amount of talk about him had stirred up too many erratic emotions.

"Can't you talk him into it?"

Meg shook her head and stared at the back of her hands.

"You're pretty good at convincing people."

"Not this time."

Kate's hand found Meg's and she gave it a quick squeeze. "Don't give up on him."

Meg shook her head again. "He's a good doctor and the town needs him."

"Maybe he'll come around." Kate studied her closely. "If I had to guess, I'd say you're in love with him."

The blunt statement didn't catch Meg by surprise. She was sure her feelings were written all over her face. "I don't want to mix business with pleasure."

Kate leaned closer and smiled. "Remember how James Dean was when I first moved to the ranch? He was all-business and so was I."

Meg blinked and felt herself smile. James Dean had fought his love for Kate. A tiny ray of hope danced inside her.

Maybe...*no*, she couldn't allow herself to count on something that might never happen. It wouldn't be fair to Steve to get involved with him if she didn't understand how he felt.

The back door opened and slammed shut, and both women looked up as James Dean marched into the kitchen.

"Everything's done for the night."

Kate gazed up at her husband as he came to stand beside her. His hand stroked her curls.

Meg's heart ached. Until now, she'd never realized how much she'd missed a family and someone to love. Her cousin had changed a lot since he'd met Kate.

There'd been a time when Meg had thought James Dean would turn into a bitter old man without any love in his life, but Kate had rerouted his course. In their case, love had created understanding—in *some* relationships love could do that.

"Is the incubator working all right?" Kate lovingly caught her husband's hand and brought it to her face, rubbing her cheek against his large fingers. "Your hands are freezing, honey. Where are your gloves?"

"Incubator's fine," he said, and sat next to Kate, his arm around her shoulders.

More envy rose to Meg's throat, and she tried to swallow back the lump growing there. Kate and James Dean worried about each other and worked together.

James Dean hugged his wife, then his attention shifted to his cousin. "You look pale. Working on another virus?" He leaned back in his chair and stretched his legs. "Your cheeks were sure rosy that day. Now your eyes look a bit swollen."

"I'm tired, that's all."

"No kidding about your eyes. You been crying?"

Meg looked down at her hands and studied her nails. She'd caught herself crying the first few days after Steve moved out, but lately, she'd steeled herself. Her house seemed so empty when she came home at night. Having him right down the road wasn't easy, either.

She shifted her gaze and found both James Dean and Kate staring at her. "I haven't cried in days."

"What're you crying for?" Her cousin's face took on a hardness, and he leaned forward.

"James Dean," Kate whispered.

He leaned closer and studied Meg. "If there's a problem, I'll talk to Steve."

"No! James Dean, please, we're not in high school. I've got enough problems with the clinic."

"Insurance big shots haven't given you any slack, have they?" Her cousin sat back in his chair, his body relaxing a little.

"No. And I haven't found anyone who's willing to relocate."

James Dean's arm slid around his wife's shoulders again. "Kate and I've been talking about what a mess Jackson's gonna be in if the clinic closes."

"Tell me about it!" Meg's heart ached with the need to see Steve again. To talk to him, share her day with him the way she knew Kate and her husband did. "Well, I'd better get home. Jenny Mc-Walsh has a fever and I told Sara to call me if the aspirin doesn't bring it down."

"You need to get some rest," Kate said.

"I will after I find the right doctor. I'm going back to Dallas tomorrow. Interview some graduating med students.'' She stood up to leave. ''Thanks for dinner.''

Minutes later Meg pulled into her driveway, parked and stepped out of her car. Clutching her jean jacket more closely around her, she shivered in the chilly night air. Fall would soon be in full swing. She leaned against her car. In an odd way, the cold was comforting.

The light from the Steve's living room splashed through his undraped windows to the ground. He'd thrown himself into the renovation of his house with the same kind of determination and fervor she'd seen when he'd helped Erin Waldron, stitched her foot and talked Charlie down from his asthma attack.

Steve Hartly never did anything halfway.

Yes, like kissing.

The thought jostled provocative memories. Intense longing for him made her entire being pulsate. *How in the world can a few memories still affect me?*

Talking to Kate hadn't helped. Meg no longer could deny she loved Steve and believed in him. But she still didn't understand how he felt. And she knew to make a relationship work she needed to do that.

Steve's shadowy image crossed in front of the glowing window. Her heart thumped and sent a rush of hot desire to every cell, and she hungrily watched him until he disappeared.

Meg turned away from the Lemon House and trudged up her driveway. She opened the kitchen door but didn't bother to turn on the light. She sat down at the table and picked up her dad's cup.

She loved Steve with all her heart.

A moment later she thought about her father and how much he'd needed someone like Steve long ago. Maybe someday Steve would see he had so much to give.

This is one I can't fix. I can't bring Steve back to medicine. He has to do that himself.

The knowledge tumbled out of her subconscious, and she pressed her lips together, feeling the pulsing of her heart.

Chapter Ten

Steve moved his right shoulder to ease the soreness, then surveyed his progress. The living room of the Lemon House looked great. Thanks to Cal and the rest of the people who had come to help, the house was almost finished.

Though Cal had had to leave early, the rest had worked from early morning until an hour ago, laughing and joking all day and accomplishing a huge amount of work. They were true friends.

Steve turned back to the front window. Headlights had flashed through the living room a few moments before. He'd heard the crunch of faraway gravel and knew Meg was home. He hadn't put shades on the windows for just that reason. This way, at least, he was aware of her comings and goings.

He knelt and pushed at the section of carpet he'd

been working on, making sure it fitted tightly at the baseboard. Straightening from his bent position, he picked up Cal's tools. He'd return them as soon as he was finished.

The new carpet looked great. Working on the house, achieving something so novel to him, had been a boost to Steve's confidence. Just this afternoon he'd called his parents to say hello. His mother had told him his father would be driving up to see him soon.

Maybe he and his father could talk. Sure, they'd discuss medicine. At the realization, Steve's gut ached. He didn't want to talk to his father about professional matters. Yet he was ready to do a lot— like make love to Meg.

The sensuous thought forced him to the window, and he looked out into the darkness. From his vantage point, he could see her front yard. A long, narrow rectangle of light usually glowed from her living room after she came home.

Tonight it was dark.

For some reason, she hadn't turned on her lights. Worrisome thoughts raced through his mind. Maybe she'd fallen in the driveway or in the house.

Or someone might have been waiting for her. He told himself that was crazy. Meg had probably decided to go straight to bed after a long day. His heart pounded with more worry. He stepped to the door and pulled it open. He had to make sure she was all right.

A moment later, Steve tapped lightly on Meg's kitchen door.

There was no answer.

He rapped harder.

Suddenly, the door flew open, and he was staring at Meg. The soft light from the kitchen outlined her lush curves, enhancing her dark hair, her eyes.

"Meg, you're here," Steve heard himself say.

"Any reason I shouldn't be?" She gently pushed on the screen and motioned him inside.

"I heard you drive in, then I didn't see a light." As he stepped into the kitchen, memories assaulted him, reminding him of their talks—of how close they'd grown. And how much he'd missed just being with Meg.

Her gaze found his and told him she'd felt the same way.

"I was too tired to turn on the lights."

"Rough day?"

"Yes. I've got a lot on my mind."

Her eyes were wide, her mouth soft, half-open. God, he wanted to hold her, feel her body next to his, against his chest. His fingers ached to play with the soft strands of hair that surrounded her face and touched her shoulders.

"It's good to see you, Steve. How's the house coming?"

Her gentle words broke into his imaginings. He reminded himself he'd only come over to check on her, make sure she was okay. Now it was time to go back to his own house. But he made the mistake of looking at her for a moment too long, and his willpower crumbled.

"The Lemon house—how're the repairs coming?" she asked again.

"Great. Fine." His mouth grew dry as he gazed at her.

"Are all the renovations finished?"

"Most. Cal, Donna and a group came over to help. The drywall's up, carpet's in. Couldn't have done it without them. They're great people."

"Yes, I know. That's what Jackson's all about— the people who live here. They wouldn't let anyone down."

"I know that now."

"Did Donna work?" A familiar troubled look crossed Meg's face.

"No. Just brought lunch. Went back to the ranch. Cal stayed. Meg, she's going to be fine."

Her fingers threaded through her thick hair, pushing it back from her face. "I know I'm overly concerned, but she does too much around the ranch. And with her family history..." Her voice cracked.

Steve crossed the space between them. He knew exactly how Meg felt. Being responsible for people's lives was a tough job. He slid his arm around her delicate shoulders.

Her familiar scent, a sensual mixture of flowers and soap, wove around him, making him almost dizzy. "Meg, she's healthy. Everything will be fine."

Meg leaned against him, her head resting on his chest.

It felt so good to hold her in his arms again. His dizziness turned into a warmth starting low in his belly and spreading throughout his entire body.

"You think so?"

"I reviewed her chart when I took over for you. She's right on schedule. You're doing everything you can," he said with confidence.

She tilted her chin up, her dark eyes shiny with wonder. "You're such a good doctor. You care. That's what's important," she said.

Her words spoke to him of hope, told him that Meg still believed in him.

Without thinking of the past or the future, Steve leaned down and touched his mouth to hers. Her lips opened, her tongue darting in and out teasingly. He responded, plunging his own tongue into her sweet mouth. They connected—with more than flesh—a fierce need joining them like links of a chain.

In answer to his demands, Meg kissed him back with a deep sensuality, combing her fingers through his hair. Then she moaned his name.

His hands traced her curves, and she responded by deepening their union. They explored each other for long moments. Then Steve pulled back. He needed to gaze at her, drink her in, take it slow.

"I want to make love to you," he whispered, unable to resist what he knew was right, and needing Meg more than anything else in the world.

Meg arched back so his lips could sear her throat with kisses. His hands smoothed over her bottom. He pulled Meg against him. They moved together, their needs and emotions making them one.

He wanted Meg.

A muffled ringing sounded in the distance, but Steve ignored it and held Meg even more tightly. The sound came again, irritating him. She pulled away gently and sighed. Steve drew her into his arms again and threaded a string of kisses across her face. "Don't answer it."

"Steve—" her whisper found his ear "—I have to." She broke his close embrace and leaned back in his arms. "The McWalshes' six-year-old has a fever. I need to check on her."

His arms unwrapped automatically, and he watched as Meg found the phone. Frustration jabbed through him, however, and he had to fight the urge to cross the space between them, take her into his arms and never let her go.

Meg is a doctor first, and everything else comes second.

She cradled the receiver and sighed.

"Emergency?" he asked.

She nibbled on her bottom lip then nodded. "I've got to go out there. Thank heavens for the well-timed phone call, right?"

"Right," Steve managed to answer. The interrup-

tion had brought them back to reality. He gritted his
teeth and tried to force the ever present need for her
out of his body. He didn't want to make her life any
more difficult. "You'll be all right driving out
there?"

"Sure. It's early yet." She switched on the small
desk light and moved silently around the kitchen,
not looking at him. "This is how my life goes. But
I won't be gone long." She shrugged.

"Be careful" was all he could say. Steve made
himself cross the kitchen and leave. He breathed in
some much-needed cool air and then walked down
the driveway.

Tonight he'd let his yearnings for Meg get the
best of him. He should have had more control. He
wasn't sure where he was going with his life right
now, and he wasn't about to make love to Meg with
his plans in turmoil.

Meg was the kind of woman who had to care
deeply about a man she made love to—she'd never
give her body without her heart.

Meg flipped down the visor to block out the late
afternoon sun streaming through her windshield. Her
body still tingled from Steve's kiss last night. She
touched her tongue to her bottom lip and sighed.
The house call hadn't taken that long, but the inter-
ruption had brought both of them to their senses.

Right now, she didn't have time to think about
Steve and how much she loved him. Pressing on the

gas pedal, she sped down the asphalt ribbon of Highway 35 toward Jackson. There were house calls to make, patients to check on. The idea of the town having been without a doctor for most of the day scared her.

Meg's biggest worry was Donna. She wasn't due yet, but after her checkup this week, Meg knew she could have her baby any day.

She gripped the steering wheel more tightly, feeling pulled in a hundred different directions. Today's trip to Dallas had been a washout. Meg's stomach tightened in a knot and her head pounded. She'd interviewed twenty doctors, and not one would be as good as Steve.

At just the thought of him, confusion welled inside her. She shouldn't have kissed him last night, but she couldn't help herself. Being in his arms made her feel wonderful, made her forget her problems for a time.

And she knew without a doubt her love for Steve was growing stronger every day.

The quiet countryside slipped by and Meg turned the radio on. Rolling her head from side to side, she tried to ease the pressure forming at the base of her neck. The tension lessened a little, but not much. Worrying about the people of Jackson was getting to her.

Meg took a deep breath and prayed she'd relax. If she didn't calm down soon, she'd be no good to anyone.

A kernel of doubt formed in her mind. *Is this the way Steve felt when he left medicine and Houston?*

Meg pushed the question away. She didn't have time to think of anything but the Jackson Clinic and what she was going to do to save it. She had to make a decision. One more time she'd ask Steve to help her. If he refused, she'd close the clinic.

The thought took her breath away and made her foot tremble against the gas pedal.

No, I have to think like a doctor—be reasonable, rational, have no mixed emotions.

She couldn't practice without medical insurance—that was crazy.

Steve Hartly was her only hope.

The next morning, carrying two full coffee cups, Meg crossed the crisp grass and headed for Steve's house. Early sunshine lit her path and warmed her back while she climbed the three steps to her neighbor's front door. She put one cup down on the railing, knocked on the door and waited.

Her heart beat in her throat as the door opened and Steve appeared, shirt unbuttoned and a pair of jeans slung low on his hips. He squinted at her.

"Sorry to bother you so early, but this is the only free time I have," Meg said quickly.

Steve held open the door and motioned her in. "No problem. I've been up for an hour."

Meg picked up the other cup, stepped into the house and glanced around the living room. "What a change!'' The Lemon House had been transformed into a comfortable home.

"I'm almost finished." He ran fingers through his hair. "I couldn't have done it without everyone's help. I'm really grateful to this town and the people who live here."

"I knew they wouldn't let you down. They're good folks. I brought you some coffee." She held out his mug.

"Thanks. I haven't gotten around to getting a coffeepot yet."

"You've only seen a little of how great Jackson's residents really are."

"I'm finding out." He moved his right shoulder back and forth. "I think I'm getting too old for this kind of work, though."

"Accident?"

"I was trying to do the drywall myself. A board hit me in the shoulder. It's nothing. It didn't bother me last night."

The kiss they'd shared the other night suddenly loomed in her memory. They'd reacted to each other like there was no tomorrow.

Meg gulped and fought her nervous energy.

After they sat at the small kitchen table, she took another sip of coffee. Steve looked relaxed, more confident. He gazed back at her.

Her face went hot with the attention, then she grew angry with herself. She'd come over to ask

Steve to change his mind, and all she could think about was falling into his arms.

He touched a loose tendril of her hair and then hooked it behind her ear. Instead of pulling his fingers back, he traced the curve of her cheek. "The other night, I really was worried about you," he said.

"I think we need to forget about the other night," Meg said quickly, not wanting to lose sight of what she'd come to say.

The tip of his index finger rubbed gently against her earlobe and sent a rush of heat throughout her body. And she knew she'd never be able to forget how she felt about Steve.

"Yeah, maybe it is better to forget about the other night," Steve said. He couldn't ignore how his fingers burned from touching her hair, her skin.

Meg blinked, then nodded. Her eyes filled with a sensual light, and the sight nearly forced Steve to stand and crush her against him.

His jeans were growing tight again. All he wanted in the world right now was to lie next to Meg and make love to her.

"I have to be very up front, Steve. I came over to talk to you. Yesterday I was in Dallas, where I used every resource possible to find another doctor. It's hopeless. Is there any chance that you've changed your mind?"

He wanted to kiss her, push all their problems away and create their own world. God, how he loved her.

"Meg, I'd like to help you, but..." Though he still couldn't vocalize what he felt, he realized he hadn't changed his mind. He needed more time. Maybe he'd never go back to medicine, and he had to be honest with Meg. "No, I can't."

She raised her chin, tilting her head a little, arching her neck. "Fine. I'll head on home." She slid back her chair and stood.

"Wait, stay, let's talk." No matter what problems lay between them, he couldn't stand for her to leave so soon. In a rush to stop her, he twisted his spine as he got to his feet, and the muscles in his shoulder suddenly convulsed. He winced.

"Is your shoulder bothering you?"

Steve lifted his arm and rotated the joint. "It's nothing."

"Come on. I know something is wrong. You might have a chipped or broken bone."

"Nah, it's nothing."

"You can't fool me. You're in pain." She was next to him before he could protest again.

"I'm—"

"I've had enough difficulties this week. Don't argue." She shook her head. "Really, doctors are the worst patients. Take off your shirt."

"Hell, I'd better be okay."

She pulled gently at his unbuttoned shirt, her fingers brushing his skin.

Steve swallowed hard. "Okay, I'm not an invalid yet, I can undress myself." He stepped back to make some space between them. That small chasm was the only thing that kept him from dragging her into his arms.

Meg watched as Steve finished slipping out of his shirt and hung it on the back of the kitchen chair. His scent reminded her of fresh air, and her thoughts were thick with memories of the kisses they'd shared over the last few weeks.

"Sit down and let me have a look," she managed to say.

"I'm telling you, Meg, it's nothing. I *am* a doctor."

"Yes, and the first rule of any doctor is not to treat yourself when you're hurt or sick." She tried to sound serious, but her heart was beating so fast. Goodness, the sight of him naked from the waist up took her breath away.

He sat in the chair she pointed to and she placed her right hand on his shoulder. Their body heat mingled, and more out-of-control heartbeats pounded against her ribs.

She told herself she needed to remain focused long enough to examine him.

In the pure morning light, she could see that all Steve's hard work on the Lemon House had honed his chest and arms to perfection. His stomach rippled with definition.

Without a thought of self-control, she drank in the sight of his well-defined waist and hips. *God, he has one hell of a body.*

"Well?"

His sexy voice sent a shiver down her spine and she pulled back. She was trembling! Determinedly, Meg wrestled with her thoughts and reactions.

A small bruise had formed beneath his smooth, tanned skin. The bruising needed to be checked.

"Something wrong?" he asked.

"No."

Meg closed her eyes for extra fortitude. She had to pull herself together. She opened her eyes and touched his shoulder again.

"There's a little bruising. Any pain?"

"Nah, not really." Steve told himself that his shoulder, at the moment, was not the problem. With Meg so close, he didn't know if he was coming or going.

"Let me check and make sure no bones are broken."

With her voice just above a whisper, he could barely hear what she was saying. "Don't worry about it. I told you I'm fine." He lifted his arm slightly.

"Let me be the judge of that."

She palmed his forearm and biceps. The warmth from her smooth hands seeped into his skin again, traveled to his heart and took his breath away.

Meg guided his arm in a circular motion and manipulated the muscles. Steve closed his eyes. The movement was a welcome diversion from what he was really feeling. He couldn't handle what was going on in his heart, head and body all at the same time.

"Does this hurt?" she asked.

"No, it's just a little sore." He gazed up at her.

She stood a few inches away, and the familiar scent of her perfume assaulted his senses again and made him more light-headed. Her hair, tangled and sexy, brushed against his arm for one sweet moment, then was gone.

"You're lucky. I think it's just bruised. Come into the office and I'll x-ray the shoulder if it keeps bothering you." Gently, she placed his arm back by his side.

She didn't move away. Her hand stroked his skin and sent passionate flames shooting through his body. He had only one thought and that was to take Meg into his arms and make love to her.

Standing next to Steve, Meg felt her senses becoming heightened. Instead of worrying about his shoulder and whether he was injured or not, she was barraged with thoughts of intimacy and sex.

Yet she couldn't risk opening up to Steve again. He made her feel so tender and defenseless, and with all her problems, she needed to be strong. Why did his closeness take away her ability to reason about Jackson and its problems—her problems?

Steve moaned very softly.

She found her fingers were still drawing circles on his skin, and she felt powerless to stop. The need for Steve was far too strong to resist. But she couldn't let this go on. She had to break the spell.

"Charlie's practicing his breathing, pretending he's Doc Steve. Kate said he hasn't had one asthma attack."

Steve stood, staring at her. "Cute little guy. Kids with asthma have it tough."

"Is that compassion in your voice?"

"Just because I decided to get out of medicine doesn't mean I lost all my empathy." His eyes narrowed with sincerity.

"I know, Steve. That's what I admire about you." The statement was as stark as a blue Texas sky on a cold day. She admired him for so many things. "Practice with me, Steve. Come work at the clinic. You'll be wonderful for the town."

His silence spoke volumes.

"I'll have to close the clinic if you won't work with me. Jackson will have to survive without a doctor."

Her statements sliced into Steve's heart. He cared about the people who lived in the small town. Total confusion enveloped him, and he shook his head. He couldn't change how he felt, but for some reason he couldn't stand to think about the clinic closing, either. He was like a kid who didn't know what he wanted. But he couldn't lie to himself or Meg.

"I'm not ready to practice medicine again, Meg. I'm not sure if I'll ever be ready. I hope you understand."

She nodded once. "I'll have to close the clinic, then. We can't go on like this. Teasing..." Her arm swept around the room. "I think it's best we stop seeing each other. You have a lot of decisions to make and so do I."

He stared at her, thinking about all the good things she represented. Hard work, dedication, strength, passion. Qualities he admired so much. But she was right. He had many things to think about.

"You're right. We both need to get our lives straightened out," he said, then wished he hadn't. But making love would just confuse them. They needed to keep perspective. Yet he knew something else was true, too.

He loved Meg Graham with all his heart.

Chapter Eleven

When Steve's doorbell rang the next day, he imagined it might be Meg. At that crazy thought, a thrill careened through him. Smiling, he pushed himself off the couch, walked to the door and swung it open.

Howard Hartly, with a serious expression, stood on the small porch.

Although glad to see his father, Steve wasn't in any mood for medical talk. "Dad, how are you?" he asked, his stomach tightening.

"Aren't you going to ask me in, Steven?"

"Sure, come in." He took a step back and his father walked through the door.

They stood in the living room facing each other.

"Some people at the hospital told me a doctor from Jackson called to inquire about your medical credentials.'' His father crossed his arms and glanced around the room. "Nice place."

"Thanks. I fixed it up. You should have seen it before. I've painted, put up drywall, laid new carpet."

"You've always been talented in many areas, Steven."

Steve stepped back. "It's good to see you, Dad. Thanks for visiting." He headed back to the couch.

The senior Hartly studied his son as he followed. He sat in the opposite corner and once more folded his arms across his large chest.

"Thanks for keeping in touch with your mother. She's missed you."

"I've missed you both. I just needed to get away."

"Everything all right?"

Steve nodded. "Yes."

"Who was the physician who called? A friend?"

"The best doctor in town." Steve leaned back and thought of Meg, wondering what she would think of his father.

"If you're thinking about returning to medicine, why don't you come back to Houston?"

Steve shook his head.

His father's arms uncrossed.

"I haven't thought about going back to Houston since…" Steve worked at not saying more.

His father turned to face him, but didn't move any closer. "I thought you might be practicing again."

"How's that?"

"The call about your credentials."

"Meg needs another physician for her clinic and..." Steve let the explanation trail off.

"And?"

"I'm not interested." They were talking superficially, as usual. Steve had never found a comfortable way to confide in his father. And his father never pushed for a deeper conversation.

"Not at all?"

Steve shook his head again. He'd hoped at one time his father had been proud that he'd become a doctor. The only time he knew Howard Hartly was happy was when they were talking about medicine. And yet when Steve quit the ER, his father hadn't said a word. He'd needed his father's counsel then.

"Smart move, asking for your help. You're an excellent physician, a damned good one."

Steve turned back. *"Was."* He waited for his father to add a disclaimer, something about how a good doctor would never quit. But the elder Hartly remained silent, his steady gaze directed straight ahead. To fight the pain in his heart, Steve drew in a deep breath.

Howard turned and faced his son. "Steven, I came here today because I wanted to explain, clear things up."

"I'm not sure what you mean. I don't want to discuss returning to medicine."

"No, no. I want to talk about us."

The words sounded alien to him. "Us?"

His father crossed his arms again. "Took me a long time to realize my stubborn ways." Howard stirred self-consciously on the couch. "I've been a fool, son. A stupid fool."

Steve stared in disbelief. His father was always the man in charge. The one who did everything right.

"Let me explain. I should have talked to you right after the incident at the hospital, but I didn't. You want to know why?"

"I have no idea." Steve had been in a deep depression at first and hadn't realized his father had cut him out of his life until later.

"Because I was raised that way. And so was my father before me and probably his father, too. Hartly men let difficult matters go. We're great at being physicians, but not parents. It's taken all the time you've been gone for your mother to convince me of that." He exhaled, placed the flat of his palms on his thighs and stared down at the carpet. "I was a father, but not much of a dad."

His honesty touched Steve.

"You were an excellent physician," his father stated firmly.

"I liked what I did. I just couldn't fight the system anymore. The insurance companies, the rules..."

"Don't get me wrong, I'm not trying to coerce

you into changing your mind. This is just a father and son talking.''

Steve remained silent, in awe of what was happening.

"Every physician, one day, has to come to the realization we're only human. We can only do so much. We have to learn that all we can do is our best, that's all we can do."

"But, Dad, I couldn't help that woman and her baby." The grief was still with him.

"Yes, I know. It was tragic, but you did as much as you could. After you left, I went to the emergency room and talked to people, reviewed records. You did everything, more than I could have done. *You're a top notch doctor.*"

"I can't forget."

"That's your best tool. You need to use that quality to help people. Don't ever *forget.*"

Meg had said almost the same thing. *You can help people who need you. Bring other babies into the world.*

Steve's head ached with confusion. Would he ever practice medicine again?

"I wasn't there for you, son. When I was your age, I fought a lot of demons, wanting to be perfect. The only thing that matters is that you care—that you have compassion." His father reached out and slapped the couch with a vengeance. "Use all of your experiences to make yourself a better doctor."

"At one time you felt like I do?" Suddenly

Steve's perception of his father changed. Maybe they weren't so far apart, after all.

Howard nodded. "I did. I got tired of the bureaucracy, too, and worried that I couldn't make a difference. I wasn't there for you when you needed me, but I will be now."

Steve stared at him. This felt good, really good. They'd never had a father-and-son talk before. Howard Hartly, M.D., had always been too busy, too involved helping other people to take time for his own family.

"Steven, you belong in medicine. Even more than I do."

Steve flinched. He didn't want to hear that from the man he respected. "I appreciate your talking to me, but..." He shrugged his shoulders.

"I believe in you." His father sat forward on the couch and put his hand on his son's arm.

"The system is screwed up. It hurts people."

"True, but it's all we have right now."

Steve remained silent, only nodding his head.

"Your mother wants you back in Houston so badly she can taste it."

Steve smiled, thinking about his mom.

"Son, we need to have a long talk. There are so many things we've never really discussed before. I want to share with you some incidents in my own career. And talk to you about coming back to Houston." He grasped Steve's shoulder, then sat back again.

"I could have done better," Steve murmured.

"We all think that at one time. You burned out. It happens to the best doctors."

His father's words touched his heart, and for the first time in a long time, Steve felt like he *was* a doctor....

Two hours later, he stood on the front step, waving goodbye to his father. They'd talked long and hard, and Howard Hartly had revealed his own concerns about the medical system. Steve had seen a part of his father he'd never realized existed. Their talk had helped him look at his feelings more clearly.

Amazed, he walked into the house and sat on the couch. His father had asked him to come back to Houston and practice with *him*.

Steve took a deep breath. He didn't want to go back to Houston...didn't want to leave Meg and Jackson. Abruptly he stood, energy bursting through every vein. He walked into the kitchen and filled a glass with water.

Meg needed him and he'd let her down. That sobering thought felt like a punch to his gut.

Yet another grim realization assaulted him. Even with his dad's support, he wasn't sure he was ready to become a doctor again.

Chapter Twelve

"Kate sent me in to pick up some medicine for the kids," James Dean announced as he walked into Meg's office.

She glanced up from a stack of patients' charts and tried to smile at her cousin. With only an hour's sleep last night, she'd been going on pure adrenaline.

"Hi, James Dean. Sandie put the samples here somewhere." She pawed through a drawer and found the white envelope. "How are the kids? Does Kate need me to stop by?"

"Nah, they're fine. Charlie picks up every germ he comes in contact with at school and brings them all home for the rest of the family to enjoy. Next, Kate'll be flat on her back and I'll be Mr. Mom."

"Don't complain. You love domesticity and you know it."

James Dean chuckled and looked across the desk. "You look like you could use a good eight hours of sleep."

Meg rubbed her forehead. "True. I made three house calls last night and managed to get to bed at five, then was up again at six." Memories of Steve and their many happy moments together had robbed her of any chance of more sleep.

"Anything critical?"

"One false alarm, diagnosed indigestion that felt like a heart attack, and—" she drew in a deep breath, held it, then exhaled "—pneumonia."

"Can I help?"

Her cousin's question warmed her. At least there was someone who cared if she slept or not.

"You okay, Mego?"

Meg gulped. "I'm closing the clinic." She leaned back in the chair and closed her eyes. The blood pounded against her temples.

"Closing?"

"The insurance company is right. Most of the time I'm walking around in a daze. I need another doctor."

"It's gonna be scary without you." James Dean got up from his chair. He volleyed the white envelope between his palms and started for the door, then turned back. "Steve hasn't changed his mind?"

"No." Usually she could put her feelings on hold

and go on, but not this time. Thoughts of Steve Hartly would always be with her.

James Dean sat down again, a sincere, worried look on his face. "So?"

I love Steve. The thought pierced her composure, and she didn't manage to conceal the fact.

"Hey, Mego, you all right?"

"Yeah, I'm…I guess…" Her voice faltered.

James Dean leaned forward. "You sure don't look okay."

She dropped her gaze to the desk and took a deep breath. She needed to gain control of her emotions. "I'm fine, really."

"Then why do you get that weird look on your face whenever I mention Steve?"

"I don't know. Maybe it's because I haven't had any sleep."

"You can't fool me. And I recall you're the one who shook me by the scruff of the neck when I was about ready to give up on Kate."

"I think *she* was about ready to give up on you."

"Whatever. But you're not as dumb as me, Meg. You love him and he loves you. That is all that matters."

"I have too many problems to think about love."

"There's always room for love, isn't there?"

The question stunned her. "He needs to find out what he wants to do and I need to—"

"You and Steve belong together—Kate and I were talking about it the other night. But you're both as stubborn as mules, with your heads stuck in the sand.''

''You just mixed your metaphors. Our relationship won't work.''

James Dean's own gaze turned stubborn. ''It'll work if you just give the relationship a chance.''

''I don't have time. I have to put the clinic first.''

''You feel so darned guilty about losing your daddy that you work too hard. Steve seems to have his own troubles. I don't know what they are but...I'm betting he'll get over his.''

''I can't worry about it.''

Her cousin shook his head. ''Sure you can. The man took your practice for a couple of days when you needed him. That was a start. He sewed up your foot.'' James Dean's gaze stayed on her. ''And what about Charlie?''

''Can we talk about something else?''

''Fine, but one more thing. If you give Steve some slack time, he'll come around. Try putting yourself in his shoes, Mego.''

Such simple advice, yet so hard to take. She rubbed her eyes.

''I don't mean to be messing around in your business, but you've buried yourself so deep in work, you've forgotten about the most important thing in life.''

She glanced up. It wasn't very often James Dean waxed philosophical.

''Yep, you forgot about love. You were smart

enough to make me see it, so why can't you see it for yourself? Love should come before anything else.''

Her cousin's words dug at her and the tightness in her throat grew.

''Steve cares about medicine and now the town,'' James Dean said, raising his voice a bit. ''You need to put him first if you love him like I think you do. Everything else will fall into place.'' He nodded, got up and walked out of her office.

Meg stared at the wall. Why did her personal life have to be so baffling? Why couldn't it be like the science she practiced, black and white? Right or wrong? Despite the worry that assailed her, her heart swelled with love for Steve Hartly.

The next morning, stark images of Jackson without a doctor woke Meg from a fitful sleep. Children getting sick, babies being born without proper medical help had filled her dreams, mixing with the growing love she was feeling for Steve.

Meg sat straight up in bed, a thin film of sweat covering her body. No, she couldn't let the people of Jackson down. She'd practice without medical insurance. Hell, she'd practice out of her house if she had to.

With relief at having made that decision, she threw back the covers, ready to get up. The phone by her bed rang, and Meg turned to answer it.

Two minutes later she sprinted to the kitchen.

Jack Smith's three kids had just come down with sore throats, and his truck's transmission was blown. She'd have to drive the fifty miles.

As she sped down the highway, Meg realized how giving up the clinic had been a ridiculous idea. She'd take the chance. Some way her plan would work.

And Steve.

She was going to tell him that she would stand by him no matter what.

Steve drove slowly up the gravel drive to Cal and Donna's ranch. He planned to return Cal's tools, then go back to the Lemon House and start working. Steve parked his car in front of the efficient ranch house, pulled the tools out of the trunk and headed for the front door.

Cal's truck was nowhere in sight, he realized, glancing around the yard. He'd leave the tools with Donna and call Cal later. The early morning sun was in its full glory, and Steve enjoyed the warmth on his face.

He felt better. His talk with his dad had freed him in a way, yet his need to be with Meg plagued his every thought.

He knocked on the worn surface of the door.

There was no answer.

Steve rapped again, then stepped back and looked around. The barn was open. He was sure Cal wouldn't leave his barn door open if he wasn't home. And Donna should be here resting. It was only days before the baby was expected.

Steve took the porch steps two at a time and headed for the barn. He'd put Cal's tools in there and close it up before he headed home.

Dust rose as he crossed the gravel drive and stood at the entry to the barn. "Hey, anyone home?" A muffled cry caught him by surprise. "Cal? Donna?" Steve edged into the barn, his gaze shifting to the left, then right.

"I'm over here."

The soft, feminine response propelled him to the first stall. Donna was sprawled on a mound of hay. Steve rushed over to her. "Donna, are you okay?"

She glanced up and smiled faintly. "Oh, am I glad to see you."

"Are you in labor?"

Before she could answer, she arched and moaned, rubbing the small of her back.

Steve's stomach tightened. He drew in a breath, yet automatically reached for her shoulders and massaged them lightly. "Donna, just take it slow, breathe, take it slow." His voice was steady, firm, and to his surprise, all his trepidation faded away.

The labor pain eased and Donna looked up at Steve. "Am I having the baby?"

"Yes, I believe so." Steve rubbed her large belly with the palm of his right hand. "How far apart are your contractions?"

"I haven't been timing them." Another pain started, and her face constricted in agony.

"You just answered my question." Steve shifted and put his arm around her shoulders. "That a girl, breathe, take it easy. Pant, like you and Cal have been practicing."

It was a blessing Meg had schooled Donna and Cal in natural childbirth.

Steve glanced around the barn as he encouraged Donna. He could see a stack of clean, thick towels in the barn office and a soft blanket hanging from a rack. All the other supplies he'd need might be found there.

From the intensity of her contractions and the short time between, Steve knew he didn't have any option about moving his patient.

Donna's last labor pain subsided, and Steve shifted his attention back to the woman. "There's no time to get you up to the house."

She smiled, her face shiny with sweat. "Goodness, I'm glad you're here. I called Meg, but she'd driven out to the Smiths' place. Sandie beeped her." Her smile faded and fear swept into her eyes. "I'm afraid, Doc. My sisters had trouble with their babies."

For a quick moment, Steve felt her fear, and panic clenched his stomach. But then he saw the trust and need in Donna's gaze. Confidence and hope built inside him, shoring him up.

"Hey, we'll do this together. Everything will be

all right. You're healthy and the baby will be, too.'' The words came from deep within his heart.

Another pain gripped Donna, and she gritted her teeth.

"You can do it. Breathe, Donna. Like you and Cal practiced—breathe and don't push." Steve spoke evenly and softly, then puffed along with his patient, rubbing her belly, feeling its tightness against his palms. When the pain subsided, he took Donna's face in his hands. "Everything's going to be all right. You trust me, don't you?"

She nodded, her eyes wide. "I know you're a fine doctor."

"Good." His heart swelled with compassion for the brave woman beside him. "I'm going to get a blanket and towels. Don't do anything till I get back."

Donna smiled weakly, pressing her hand to her sweat-soaked forehead.

Steve ran to the office and grabbed the supplies. He was excited and elated all at the same time. When Meg arrived, they could get Donna and the baby to the house, or to a hospital if need be.

The last thought stunned him for a split second, but he shook it off and remembered Meg's words. He'd do his job, use his expertise. He cared—that was all that mattered.

Back at Donna's side, he spread out the blanket next to her. "Let's get you comfortable."

Steve helped her ease onto the blanket. Donna

lifted her head and then limply lay back. He took off his shirt and mounded it like a pillow under her head, then knelt next to her.

"I need to check you."

She nodded.

She was fully dilated and ready. Donna moaned and her face tightened. Another contraction. Steve glanced at his watch and rubbed the woman's ankles. "You'll be holding your baby in your arms soon. Ready to be a mama?"

Donna barely nodded. "Is everything gonna be all right with the baby?" Once again her eyes filled with terror.

Steve gripped her hand in reassurance. "You let me look after that. Everything is going to be fine. And if the baby looks like you, well, it's going to be one pretty child."

Another pain gripped Donna's entire body, and they rode it through together.

"Oh, goodness, Doc. I feel different."

"With the next contraction, I want you to push." Steve readied the towels. Determination filled his heart and soul.

Donna pressed her mouth in a firm line and closed her eyes.

Steve could feel her abdomen tightening again as another contraction seized her.

"I have to push," she cried, and opened her eyes wide. "Here comes another one."

Steve knelt between Donna's knees. "Good.

You're doing a great job.'' Anticipation filled his heart. He was ready to be a doctor again.

Donna screamed.

"Good, next contraction, I want you to push again, then grab your knees, take a deep breath, hold it.'' Steve could see the baby's head crowning.

At the next contraction, Donna leaned forward, her face contorted with the effort.

"Push, push with all your might,'' Steve commanded. "Push hard. The baby's head's crowning. Push! You're almost there.''

Fifteen minutes later, Steve took the baby girl from Donna, wrapped her in a fresh towel and gazed at the child he'd just brought into the world.

Cally Bradford, minutes old, possessed a perfect heart-shaped face.

And Steve felt at peace with the universe.

The baby yawned, her tiny mouth a picture of perfection.

"You're a sleepy little gal. Well, I can understand why. You've done a lot of hard work. But you did a good job.'' Steve stroked the baby's smooth cheek.

Meg's words rang in his thoughts: *Bring other babies into the world, help other women...*

"Thanks, Doc. I don't know what I would have done if you hadn't come along. I owe you so much.''

"Nah, I owe you.'' Steve shifted his gaze to Donna. She was fine, and in a day or two, she'd be on her feet.

Her hand found his forearm. "You're a good doctor."

The soft words danced in his heart, and Steve smiled at his patient. Compassion and hope wove their way through him, filling his whole being. There was no denying it.

He was a doctor again.

Meg ran into the Bradford barn, out of breath, her heart pounding. Searching the area, she saw Steve kneeling beside Donna with a bundle cradled against his bare chest. Her breath caught in her throat and she said a quick prayer.

"Steve, I drove as fast as I could to get here." The huge smile on his face told her she didn't need to ask if mother and baby were all right.

"We handled it, didn't we, Donna?" Steve gazed down at his patient and then back to Meg. Confidence and joy glowed from his face.

"Looks like everybody's fine," she said. A wave of pride and love washed over her. She crossed the small space to mother, baby and doctor.

Donna looked at Steve and her baby, then shifted her attention to Meg. "I couldn't have had better care, Meg—only you. My baby is beautiful. Cal will be so pleased we have a girl. He didn't say so, but I know he wanted a little girl." Donna closed her eyes for a moment, then opened them. "Steve's the best doctor anybody could have."

Meg nodded and looked at Steve. Hope and promise exploded in her heart.

Four hours later she was sitting at her kitchen table, coffee cup in hand. Steve was in the very same place he'd sat the night they'd met.

A hint of crisp air edged through the screen door and floated to Meg. She shifted her gaze back to Steve, and the sight of him in her kitchen pushed her breath back in her throat.

She finally found her voice. "You did a wonderful job with Donna and the baby." She stared at him for what seemed like an eternity. He looked so different, yet the same.

"Thanks. Donna's a brave woman. She made it pretty easy."

"I need to go back and check on them tonight."

His right hand found hers, and he massaged her palm with his thumb. "If you don't mind, I'd like to check on them myself."

Her heart stilled. "Want me to come along?"

"If you can, it'd be nice, but if you're busy, I can take the house call myself."

She gazed at Steve. A warm, happy feeling washed over her. His eyes held the gleam of certainty, and she experienced a heated sensation rising from low in her belly.

"Great," she whispered.

"You think so?"

"Yes."

He nodded and smiled. "Today felt really good." He stood without letting go of her hand. "We need to talk."

"We do?" Tears welled at the corner of her eyes, and her throat start to burn.

His hands found her shoulders, and all her worries melted with his tender touch.

"Yes. Will you come into the living room where we can get comfortable?"

She sat on the couch next to him, and again he took her hand in his. For a long moment, he didn't say a word. They sat next to each other, their thighs touching, her hand clasped in his. They were breathing together, their chests rising and falling at the same time.

He let her hand go and brought his finger to her chin. Their gazes locked and she waited. Deep down she knew what he was about to say. She'd always known Steve Hartly was a fine doctor.

"Does the offer still stand for the position at the Jackson Clinic?" His voice was husky with emotion, yet strong, determined.

"Are you ready? I don't want to push you. We can take it slow. We can work things out as long as we have each other."

Steve nodded. "I'm ready. Knew it this morning when I delivered the baby. I want to be with you, help you. I want to be a doctor. We can help each other, believe in each other. I love you, Meg, with all my heart."

Her eyelids fluttered shut, and her entire body relaxed.

At last, at long last.

She opened her eyes, her heart pounding. "I love you, too."

His sweet breath brushed against her skin, then his mouth found her lips and caressed them lightly. She shut her eyes and sighed against his mouth as she leaned into him. Their time together was so precious.

He kissed her tenderly at first, and she returned his kisses. Tangling her fingers in his hair, she pulled him closer. Their kisses lengthened as their tongues danced playfully. His fingers stroked her face and throat, and both of them rejoiced in the taste and touch.

Without words, but exquisitely, they relayed their needs and feelings. And Meg knew they'd be with each other in everything they did.

Finally, Steve gently pulled away. She sat nestled against his strong chest, her head resting on his shoulder.

He tipped up her face so he could gaze directly into her eyes, his thumb massaging her jawline. "I realized today I'll always be a doctor no matter what. And we'll fight the problems together. With our love we can do anything."

"Good. I need you, Steve."

"Not just at the clinic?" The question was punctuated by the heated look growing in his eyes.

"Not just at the clinic. I love you." She spoke over the pounding of her heart.

He took in a deep breath. "I love you."

Although already said, the words sounded new and fresh, and caught her by surprise. There was no doubt in her heart that this was a forever kind of love.

His fingers caressed her shoulders as he brought her to him. "Meg," he whispered.

"Oh, Steve." Her arms wrapped around him, and she hugged him. She nuzzled her face against his throat. His scent rose around her and wove its spell. Pulling back a little, she gazed directly into his eyes. They'd turned the smoky brown she loved so much.

"No matter what happens, we'll survive it together." She said the words and they gave her such a feeling of release. She was finally free to love the man who'd captured her heart.

"We will." He wrapped his arms around her, holding her tightly. "You always believed in me."

"Something told me you were the one."

"Ah, darling." He groaned and drew her closer.

She relaxed. They melted into each other, their love growing stronger with every breath. She trembled against his rock-hard body, and he kissed her with a fervor that revealed his yearnings.

"What are we going to do about the Lemon House?" he whispered, drawing his lips away from hers.

"The Lemon House?" Her swollen mouth felt naked without his.

"We shouldn't keep both. We'll have to choose one or the other. I vote for the Lemon House."

"What?"

"When we get married. With two houses, we'll have to sell one."

"Get married?" she asked, and couldn't stop the grin forming at the corners of her mouth.

His fingers found her hair and tangled in it while he gazed down at her. "Will you marry me? I just assumed that since I love you and you love me, we'd get married."

His trusting nature grabbed at her heartstrings and reminded her why she loved the man who held her. They were taking some giant steps, but she didn't mind in the least. "Yes, I'll marry you."

His smile grew.

She kissed his lips, then his eyelids, and trailed back to his mouth again. Her heart had waited a long time for Steve Hartly.

*   *   *   *   *

Look Who's Celebrating Our 20th Anniversary:

"Happy 20th birthday, Silhouette. You made the writing dream of hundreds of women a reality. You enabled us to give [women] the stories [they] wanted to read and helped us teach [them] about the power of love."

—*New York Times* bestselling author
Debbie Macomber

"I wish you continued success, Silhouette Books....
Thank you for giving me a chance to do what
I love best in all the world."

—International bestselling author
Diana Palmer

"A visit to Silhouette is a guaranteed happy ending,
a chance to touch magic for a little while....
It refreshes and revitalizes and makes us feel better....
I hope Silhouette goes on forever."

—Award-winning bestselling author
Marie Ferrarella

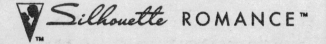

Silhouette ROMANCE™

VIRGIN BRIDES

Join
Silhouette Romance
as the New Year brings new
virgin brides down the aisle!

On Sale December 1999
THE BRIDAL BARGAIN
by Stella Bagwell (SR #1414)

On Sale February 2000
WAITING FOR THE WEDDING
by Carla Cassidy (SR #1426)

On Sale April 2000
HIS WILD YOUNG BRIDE
by Donna Clayton (SR #1441)

Watch for more **Virgin Brides** stories from
your favorite authors later in 2000!

VIRGIN BRIDES
only from

Silhouette®
Where love comes alive™

Available at your favorite retail outlet.

Visit us at www.romance.net

SRVB00

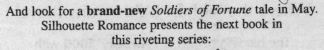
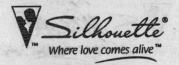